Pinprick

STORY
OF A
CHILD CANNIBAL

SCÁTH BEORH

Pinprick

related books by

Scáth Beorh

Thyme for Nightmares

Haunted by Benevolence

Hollow Boy

Horror & The Christian

The Vampires of Dreach Fola

Twelve House
2019

Pinprick

foreword by the author

I began writing *Pinprick* during a particularly terrible time of a particularly terrible year while I was living (somewhat) in a particularly terrible part of the Mid-Atlantic States known as the 'Rust Belt,' terrible as that may sound. Even though I made my abode at 1135 North Negley Avenue, a turn-of-the-century brown brick mansion haunted by two spirits of very different personalities from one another—one saintly, the other terrible—still I desperately needed to escape my self-wrought terrible surroundings. So, my 'happy place' being Ireland since I was a boy, and even moreso after I lived there as a rover for a year, there I ran—not expecting to come face-to-face with a loveable Dubliner psychopath. Who *is* this child really? I only have a vague idea, though it has been a bit over a decade since she and I were first introduced. Some may see in her Anna from Fynn's classic, others may find an inverted (or even perverted) Alice Liddel, or even Red Riding Hood—and the truth is that all of these literary characters, and several more, have informed my writing through the years. Yet, Charlotte 'Pinprick' Proorice is a new character to the mythopoetic world. She is somebody quite different from any you have met before in real life (God forbid!), in a book, or in film or animation—though she does share a few personality traits with bad girls Rhoda Penmark from *The Bad Seed*, Lenore the Cute Dead Little Girl, and Esther from *Orphan* (appearing a year after I wrote *Pinprick*.)

Listen to Charlotte. I do. She has taught me a great deal about life, perceptions, and, yes, even love. And beside all that, she will have you laughing out loud at cold-blooded murder. No? Oh, you will laugh alright. Best not to make her angry.

Scáth Beorh
January 2019

1

Murder in the Kingdom

A little girl smiled at me through her narrow mansion
window, her big eyes glistening like carrion beetles in
the morning sunshine. Her fingers and the stone
windowsill where she stood were smeared with fresh
blood. She had killed something, but her features
showed a lunacy that would send her to relatives if what
she had slain was human, and give her a slap on the
wrist if it was only her hound.

It turned out to be human— and it was my lot in life
to be hired by the house steward, a Mr. Renault, as the
child's personal coachman. My first assignment, the
following morning, was to drive Charlotte from her
home in Rathmines, Dublin through the Wicklow
Mountains to her paternal uncle's manor in Corsillagh. It
would be a long day's journey forcing us to pass through
Gleann na Gruagh, a gloomy wood haunted by
highwaymen and other denizens of low social esteem.
Under no circumstance whatever was I to allow her to
exit the four-in-hand (her privy needs while traveling to
be met with a chamber pot). I dozed an hour at most that
night, my mind unable to extricate itself from wondering
who the babe had axed to death that sunny morning.

†

As one may imagine, when we reached the darkest portion of the glen we were indeed waylaid and told to *stand and deliver*, for, the ruffians stated in no uncertain terms, it was our money or our lives. Charlotte swung open the door of her coach and smiled, and the masked highwaymen smiled with their eyes, taken aback at her sweetness. She then drew two flintlock pistols and slew them who had hailed us so boldly, a ball entering an eye-socket of one, the heart of the other.

'Pinprick!' I cried, not yet discerning the origin of my new name for the child. 'Get back in! *Quickly!* They were not the only two cutthroats who live here!'

'I like that you call me 'Pinprick,' Mister Coachman.'

'It is only that— well I believe it is that— it is as if you are like the painful prick of a pin.'

'Shall I get you a thimble then?' Charlotte swung herself back into her seat and slammed the door shut. 'I have a crossbow and full quiver, Mister Coachman. What do you have up there?'

'Nothing to your concern!' I snapped the reins so hard all four horses whinnied in anger. I figured now why I had been sent on the precarious journey alone. No need for extra servants when not required!

'I don't like mean people, Mister Coachman. You should be nice to me. My fingers do bad things to people

7

who speak harshly. To me.'

'So I hear,' I whispered, hoping she couldn't hear me.

'I heard you,' she said.

✝

Inexplicably, we escaped the woodland without further incident. We were moving along at a fair clip when, to the curdling of my blood, I registered a piercing scream which nearly unseated me. It was followed by a 'Halt!'

Did I halt? Of course I halted. My father went to his grave providing me with an education, which included knowing when I was out of my depth with *terrible enfants.*

'*There once was a man from Kilkennyyy,*' Charlotte sang as she relieved herself behind a spiny blackthorn, '*who thought he would never get anyyy—*'

I plugged my ears with my forefingers and closed my eyes. This was not happening to me. *This was not happening to me.*

'Listen to my rhyme, Mister Coachman.'

'Must I, Pinprick?' I heard myself beg.

'If you choose not,' the wee murderess replied as she brushed my sleeve with fingers still bloodstained from the morning before. *Why hadn't someone washed her hands? God in Heaven!* I begged my guardian angels to guide me safely to her awaiting uncle, being Squire Proorice. (An outrider had gone ahead with the revolting news.) I suddenly felt an indomitable celestial presence, which indeed was comforting, and my belief remained constant that God will not put upon his children any more than we can bear. But why had I been chosen, of those with far better credentials (cold-blooded murderers, for example), to escort a miniature Elizabeth Bathory! Surely this was another instance, as with Job, where the Devil had wagered with God concerning my ability to endure the unthinkable—and the Creator had accepted the challenge!

'Mister Coachman?'

'Yes, Miss Proorice?'

'Please call me 'Pinprick.''

'Yes, Miss Pinprick.'

'*Pinprick* by itself will do.'

'Right. *Pinprick*. What can I do for you?' I opened the coach door and released the stairs for her.

'Well—' she replied as she rolled her eyes, 'I'm hungry, and the basket of food prepared for me is not to my liking. I don't care for soda bread and apples. Apple pie is nice, and apple butter and apple tarts and tortes and tandrageny, but apples by themselves— no, thank you. No fruit, really, is to my liking. I much prefer chewy, raw—'

'Stop! I need no more detail! But, tandrageny? What is tandrageny?'

'Tandrageny is a dessert of my own creation, served only at birthdays—and odd ones at that. I shall make you some for your birthday, providing you are nice to me in the meantime, and are having an odd one. Now, I am hungry, as I said, and these apples are for the birds. Or the horses or squirrels, but not for me, thank you.'

My blood went icy. This meant that we had to stop at Kilmacullagh, which was only down the way, and purchase whatever would be to her heart's delight—if we could find it available, which was not likely. I was also puzzled about the 'odd birthdays,' not certain whether Charlotte meant odd numbers or peculiar situations.

'Mister Coachman, I wish to use my crossbow and kill something to eat. Like Robin Hood did.'

I was suddenly light-headed so that I fell against the lacquered coach, the sweat on my ungloved hand causing me to slip quickly along the surface so that my next contact was an eyebrow on the solid brass lamp.

'Mister Coachman? Did you see something that frightened you?' Charlotte snapped her head to gaze into a nearby stand of gorse. '*Ooooo!* You're bleeding!'

'Yes, as a matter of fact I *did* see something frightening,' I replied, trying to staunch the seepage of blood with my kerchief.

'What was it? What did you see that terrified you?' She bounced up and down on her toes, an unsettling glee in her voice.

Not answering her, which made her pinch her full lips together and glare at me, I found strength enough to help her back to her seat, and to find mine. It would have only been a few more leagues and we would have arrived at the family manor, safe if not sound. But now we needed to stop again so that she could kill something. What would she kill? And how would we cook it? We would be all night reaching our destination at this rate, and my position with the Proorices would most likely be lost. I may even be put into custody for kidnapping, and if that were to happen, I, a man of low estate, would certainly be at least imprisoned.

We drove on.

'Stop at the wee wood near Kilmacull, Mister Coachman!' Charlotte's sudden cry sent sharp slivers of ice down my spine. She then thrust her head out of the open window. 'We're near there now. I can tell by the sweeter air. And, we just passed Bloodland.'

I couldn't help myself. 'Bloodland?' I cried, trying to direct my voice backward at full gallop.

'It's nothing, Mister Coachman.' We rode on in silence as I reflected upon driving straight past 'the wee wood near Kilmacull,' but then considered that a crossbow arrow could easily pierce the roof of the coach.

'Good thinking,' she said.

I froze where I sat.

†

'Here, Mister Coachman. Pull over here! See the wee little wood?'

Seeing a smallish copse of oak growing in front of farmland, I said not a word as I slowed the team, dismounted, and prepared to water and feed them. I was glad it was near Midsummer, for we had many hours of light left though my pocket watch showed half past five.

'Do you like my crossbow, Mister Coachman?'

I turned and saw that the medieval weapon which had singly altered the face of warfare in that woebegone era was now pointed at my privy parts and loaded with a deadly-looking bolt. I hopped away like a man on fire and hid myself behind the nearest oak tree.

'I wasn't going to shoot you, Mister Coachman.'

'What were you going— going to do then? *Frighten me to death?*'

'Maybe. And careful with your tone. I have funny fingers. They like to dance.' Then she tromped off into the wood, likely glad they had dressed her in knickerbockers.

†

The team 'ostled properly, I climbed back into my
seat and, shaking like sheep fuzz in a breeze, packed my
long clay tavern pipe with a rich cherry tobacco, lit it,
and tried to relax.

'*Mister Coachman!*'

I do not remember taking myself down from the four-
in-hand. Nor do I remember running into the wood.
After Charlotte's scream colored the surrounds like a
nightmare, my first recollection is seeing the handsome
lad crawling toward me, his eyes bulging as he gasped
for air, a crossbow bolt piercing his neck at the left
jugular.

'I got one!' cried Charlotte with the glee of Christmas
Morn. 'One of the shepherd lads! Oh, will he be tender
enough to eat? I hope I haven't made a mistake, Mister
Coachman.' With her words she fired another arrow
from the evil contraption, this one squarely entering his
heart. He fell with a thump to the dewy grass.

'*Mmmm*, smells wonderful, doesn't it? I so love the
scent of freshly spilled blood. They wouldn't let me eat.'

I had the crossbow in one hand and Charlotte's right
arm in the other, dragging her by the collar of her
waistcoat back to the coach. How I accomplished it I do
not to this day know, but soon I had the child tied
securely and placed in her seat. Later I wished I had
gagged her, but chose not to stop yet again to risk some

kind of mishap such as a bite to my own jugular, or perhaps the employment of some hidden weapon I was unaware of.

†

Two sizeable footmen, several servants, and Charlotte's uncle all appeared as if they greeted the 'Ooser' itself as we arrived. When I was ushered into the Great House, for fear that I was dying, a quick glimpse into an outsized wall mirror showed me the reason for their pallid complexions. Though I knew the reflected figure to be me, the green skin and disheveled hair of a lunatic were completely incongruent with my usual demeanor.

'Sir!' Squire Proorice whispered as he waved away all servants but his footmen— whom I noticed were uncharacteristically armed. 'What is the meaning of your arrival here with my niece?'

'Arrival?' I was still very much dazed.

'Aye! Were you not properly briefed?'

'What— should I have been briefed about, sir?' I managed to ask.

Squire Proorice looked to his footmen and the few family members who had entered the room. He then turned back to me.

'Based upon your, ah, *curriculum vitae*, shall we say,' the rich man replied, 'you were hired to perform a certain *service* for the family.'

'I am afraid I do not follow you, sir,' I said. 'I have done as requested. The child is quite safe, though I do apologize for her being bound. I can explain.'

The gentleman closed his eyes as beads of sweat erupted over his now-pallid countenance.

'Are— you not John Copper, newly released from Dublin Castle gaol to, shall we say, *serve* the Proorices with a most necessary but particularly unsavory duty?'

'Copper? *Copper*, did you say? No sir, my surname is *Coppe*. I am John *Coppe*.'

'Oh God in Heaven! There seems to have been a terrible mistake. The rush and bustle of yesterday, surely. All of the confusion—*the tragedy of it all*. May— may I ask, Mr. Coppe, how came you to be hired?'

'A reputable reference made an appointment for me a fortnight ago.'

'That damned steward Renault!' The Squire turned and glared at his footmen, who flinched and fumbled for their failing dignities. 'Renault's infernal loss of memory has caused us far too much pain this time round!'

'Sir,' I said with a quavering voice, 'if I may be permitted. I am quite sure that— that I do *not* understand what has happened. Mr. Renault was quite cordial in his correspondence, if obviously a bit flustered. Might I inquire into the particulars, even a wee bit, in order to clear my own mind?'

Squire Proorice again looked about him, and, I assume, receiving a familial consolation invisible to me, perhaps because of my own bedraggled state, turned back and placed his large hand on my shoulder.

'You, my man—or I should say the murderer John Copper—were hired to dispatch that devil Charlotte somewhere on the highway from Dublin.'

'Not my sweet Pinprick,' I whispered nearly inaudibly.

'Say you something, Master Coppe?'

†

Having with a purloined bag of coin currency made amends to the clans of the two murdered thieves (one of which, ironically, had been John Copper deciding not to make himself present for his Proorice Manor assignment once released from gaol for that particular duty), Charlotte and I today abide in a comfortable stone cottage hidden in the olden oaks, ash, and beech of *Gleann na Gruagh.* Though my education and my father's memory may be sullied by my present actions, I could not see the disturbed child assassinated over a condition of mind completely out of her control.

We did well for ourselves when the affluent traveled through that perpetually shadowed woodland.

Furthermore, Charlotte taught me to fashion and fletch crossbow bolts, using Antrim flint for their points.

2

A Regrettable Event

'I don't *want* to wear my hair in pigtails, Mister Coachman!'

'But Pinprick, my dear,' I pleaded. 'We are highwaymen now. The tree branches—'

'No! I like my hair down! You are making me angry, Mister Coachman!'

My very last desire was to make Charlotte angry. I abhorred the thought, for when I had last enjoyed her lost temper, I also enjoyed a painful swipe of her rapier to my right cheek, realizing with the sting that she was sinister of hand as well as sinister of mind.

'Why did you save me from my Uncle Gallian, Mister Coachman? I know my family gave you a position so as to kill me. Why did you save me?'

I sat on a nearby mossy stone, so weak became my knees at such candid query.

'Well, I— I feel that you have great value. And so feeling, though I disagree with your love of slaughter, my world view cannot allow me to see anyone innocent die simply because— simply because—'

'Simply because they are insane? As am I, Mister Coachman?'

I could not answer. I could do nothing but gaze into

her fathomless eyes, searching for some chance of light. I discovered none. No, Charlotte was utterly dead of heart, yet in some way capable of remaining lively of soul, perhaps because she was yet but a child carrying none of the baggage so easily shouldered by those of us ostensibly older and wiser.

'Answer me, Mister Coachman!'

'Madam! Your tone! I ask that you relieve yourself of your anger toward me and communicate in a gentler way. We are, after all, comrades in crime.'

'True that, Mister Coachman. True that.' She then began to walk toward me at such a slow pace, her feral eyes directed into mine, that I could not help but be horribly reminded of tales I had heard from associates having sailed the Caribbean and surrounding waters— yarns of morbid slavery through the use of black sorcery, with resulting thralls known as *nzambi*.

'What will we do today?' Charlotte asked me as she sprung herself onto my boots, bouncing up and down upon them with such force that, until I lifted her into the air, I feared the toes of them would be crushed, and so, eternally ruined.

'A thousand wrong dancers made me born!' she cried as she squirmed to be let down. I thought in the moment that maybe I was not, after all, in the presence of a mad child, but in the perverse court of a demented poetic genius.

'Tell me more,' I heard myself say as she placed a newly-fletched bolt into her crossbow and took aim at a lone raven picking at a crust of soda bread I had dropped for it earlier.

'*Ha!* I would never kill a raven!' Charlotte swung her weapon toward a nearby peregrine falcon and, in the twinkling of an eye, skewered it to the ash limb where it rested. 'Practice makes perfect.'

As the unfortunate creature cried piteously and slapped and fluttered its beautiful wings in a furious attempt to maintain its ebbing life, I found myself only able to keep my cold, stony seat while shaking my head from side to side as if I had suddenly become mentally aberrant. A child does not deserve to die for its sins, no matter how miscreant.

'What are you thinking about, Mister Coachman?' She startled me from my solemn reverie.

'Oh, nothing of import, my sweet girl.' I wiped with my shirtsleeve pearls of perspiration from my brow.

'You sweat like a man soon to be hanged, yet it is quite cool out,' Charlotte observed. 'Have I upset you, Mister Coachman?'

'What have you gotten us for supper?' I begged in attempted diversion of the theme at hand. 'You've been away alone for quite a spell this morning. And, why do you now plait your hair into pigtails?'

'I *like* pigtails. You should pigtail *your* hair.'

'I would rather not.'

'You are making me angry, Mister Coachman.' She unsheathed her dirk from its bejeweled ebon scabbard and fell toward me in full dead weight. I escaped this antic of terror with but a slight scratch on the outside of my hand near my palm, made by the point of the blade as I sought to protect my vitals from its slicing power. The dainty Dubliner fop, the Lord Harlan, only the day before had not been so lucky as I, and had lost his left lung, and thus undoubtedly his life in later hours, during Charlotte's surprise knavery thought, until the reprehensible moment of truth, to be but a convivial childish jest on her part. Nevertheless, we relieved His Lordship and his fellow travelers of their foodstuff and accoutrements, and also of their casket of currency (meaning to buy necessities from those who dare venture this horrid glen for to trade. In my view, only the haughty rich deserved to be relieved of their purses. Distressingly, robbery wasn't high on my young murderess's list of reasons for highway robbery.)

I refuse to kill save that we eat, and sought to teach Charlotte that she need not slay one or more of every hapless party traveling through our 'neck of the woods,' as went the saying concerning such darkened abodes strewn like berries here to there across the Isles. But my wee girl was a hard one, for she insisted that she must smell human blood, and taste of human flesh, or she would surely die. This supposed desire of hers was, of course, part and parcel of her disease, and so I could but pray for her, and for myself, and hope that my guidance for her was not cut short in one of her unpredictable berserks.

'Pigtails! Mister Coachman! *Pigtails now!*'

'But—'

Again was drawn her rapier, and this time I found it bobbling upon my throat.

'Right, then,' I replied, and I proceeded to take out my ponytail for to transform it into pigtails. I had not finished the work when I felt Charlotte's nine-year-old fingers massaging my scalp, seeking to part my hair down the middle so as to make the change more readily accomplished.

'Are you old enough to be my father, Mister Coachman?'

'Most definitely, Charlotte. A youthful father, indeed, but a father notwithstanding.'

Fingernails tore into my scalp like hot thorns. My instinct led me to knocking her hands away with my forearms, which caused her to jump and run, only to race back toward me with a brace of loaded pistols aimed at my eyes.

'You called me Charlotte! I don't like that, Mister Coachman! I don't like that very much at all!'

I sat bewildered, my loosened hair straggling down over my cheeks like so many dusty cobwebs. Would I ever be able to know comfort with this child I already loved so much? Would she ever trust me? Likely not, I reckoned, and so, to calm her, I spoke her new name— *Pinprick*—over and over in ever-softened tones until she uncocked her two pistols, slipped them into her wide leather belt, and knelt next to me on some old swaddling clothes. When she lay her head onto my knee, I began to weep.

'Please don't cry, Mister Coachman. No! Don't cry! I forbid you to cry!' And with those words I saw her wipe tears from her cheeks.

Sweet and hellish was my Charlotte, and I both adored her and dreaded every moment of my life with her. Yet, I knew that her malady would not allow her to transcend the *thesaurus terrorem* in which she reveled. Did she truly enjoy those murky places of the mind? I could only assume that she did indeed, knowing not peaceable praxis from destructive thought and action. I am quite sure—knowing what I know now—that the world seemed to her a strange place where only her weapons of warfare gave her validation— where only her killing gave her a place to stand amongst mankind.

'Pigtails!'

And with that, in minutes my head was transformed, according to my pocket glass, into something altogether morose.

'Pinprick please—'

'No! Hush and eat your falcon! I *like* your Red Indian pigtails. *Wear them!*'

✝

That evening, after we rested nestled within a deep wood of ancient oaks, Charlotte disappeared. I assumed that she went to the top of the eastern hill where grows a hefty copse of ash, and where fairies are alleged to abound, but when she came back dragging behind her the dead lamb, I knew she had visited the northwestern 'hidden' glen nuzzling quietly against grazing land— a wondrous place of bluebells and the most delectable whisperings a person could ever wish to hear.

'Supper!' Charlotte cried, elated. 'With the mint sauce *you* will make!'

'O God,' I replied, for it was just then that along the path behind her came two strapping shepherds carrying blunderbusses, righteous indignation painted across their faces like the American red savages I had read so much of— and since, oddly enough, have met in person.

'Ho there!' the older of the two men called to us. 'Ye

there, colleen!'

'Ye have our lamb we call *Oolie*,' hollered the younger, 'and though ye've slain him, we lay claim to him yet!'

I stood from where I sat beneath a favorite tree, yet in my standing I sought to present myself as inoffensively as possible, so as to not see my last moments on Earth over the death of a mere sheep, named or unnamed. And so, my feet crossed over each other, my hands palms-out as if in great question of the situation, my head shaking from side to side as if in serious bewilderment of the scene playing out before me, I spoke. 'My dear sirs. I see that you have been introduced to my poor daughter Charlotte, stricken since birth with *gealtachta*.'

'You called me *Charlotte* again, Mister Coachman! That makes me very angry with you!'

The two men halted as if stopped by an unseen opposition, a mixture of both sorrow and horror first in their eyes and then racing across their countenances like a flood.

'*Ach! Gealtachta!*' said the elder after a moment. 'May God have mercy upon ye, child. And upon *ye*, kind sir. I suppose the babe has required your locks to be found in girlish pork-tails? Such a good-hearted father ye must be.'

'Aye, the Good God bless ye both then,' added the

younger. As he tapped the side of his head with two fingers, his brother replying with a forefinger tap to his nose, both men turned and trudged away, apparently exhausted from their search for Oolie.

'What does *gealtachta* mean, Mister Coachman?' Charlotte broke the legs of the lamb at his knees and began skinning him with her hunting knife. 'I had a fluffy cat once called Hannibrithal. It was her magical name. Her first name was Hissy. Is *gealtachta* a magical word? Does it mean that I'm a good girl?'

Tears welled into my eyes at her pure innocence. 'Aye,' I replied. 'It means that you are a good girl, Pinprick. A very good girl.'

I was loathe to relate to her the true meaning of the word, for it was one thing for her to call *herself* insane, but it would have been quite another, I believe, for me to agree with her. In this instance I was not frightened for my life with her, but rather frightened for her own mental safety, precarious thing that it already was.

My leg of lamb, roasted with wild garlic and herbs over an oaken fire and sprinkled with the perfect amount of salt, proved perfectly gorgeous. I do admit that I was forced to turn away as Charlotte pushed the animal's hot eyeballs into her mouth and popped them like ripe grapes. I asked her to please eat his brains out of my sight, which she happily did as she hung by her knees from a low tree branch, her two long pigtails dangling like ivy vines. 'I was going to kill those shepherds,' she confessed between mouthfuls. 'They should be glad they were nice to us. I'm sorry, though, that I didn't get to taste them. I've found that I quite like shepherd.'

3

The Woodmaster

I must confess that I was torn about my accidental foray
into the life of a highwayman, no matter its romanticism,
and whether or no the declaration be true that such
employment finds its origin in displaced Anglo-Saxon
gentry. In my most adventurous of dreams never did I
imagine myself a cutthroat. Allow me to quickly say that
I did not actually cut throats. I did not hurt our victims in
the least way. Charlotte dispatched enough for the both
of us, I am horrified to report. All attempts of mine to
retard her actions proved themselves fruitless. She was,
as is said, a 'bad seed,' and though I searched my soul
and all of the collective wisdom of our present age, and
of ages long gone, I knew not what to do in regard to her
violence except, of course, to pray for her soul—and my
own sanity. Her capriciousness, though, startled me the
most about her. Surely her privileged life at home among
so many attending servants had, though often damaging,
not brought her to such ruin? What had occurred there?
What was it about her Uncle Gallian? I prayed for
Charlotte that she accept direction from me, but my
prayers were not presently being answered— at least to
my limited understanding. Her continuance along the
path of murderous assault did not bode well, I am afraid,

for a pleasurable life of romantic pastoral bliss.

†

'Talk!'

'Pinprick! You startled me!'

'He won't talk!'

I looked up from my newly-acquired and already beloved volume of sonnets by William Shakespeare, only to see a beautiful red squirrel held out by Charlotte at arm's length. The animal seemed friendly enough, and I realized that she must have tamed him over a period of months, otherwise he would not have allowed her to hold him.

'He won't talk to me!'

'But my dear girl!' I replied, alarmed. 'He is a *squirrel*. He has his *own* language. He doesn't *know* yours.'

'But *my* language is the *true* language. It is the one we use to acquire our food and clothing and everything else that we need. *He should know that!*'

'Dear heart—*oh, Charlotte!* You are hurting him!'

'He's trying to bite me! He knows he is wrong! He knows he should be speaking English, not stupid squirrel language!'

'Please. Put him down. Let him go. Is he not your friend?'

Instead, Charlotte took his head in her fist and

twisted it round with a crack. Her pet squirrel was now a
dead squirrel.

'He shouldn't have been so naughty.' She took him
by his long tail and, dragging him along the floor, she
left our cottage. Later, thinking I heard her weeping, I
went to the door, only to find her swinging the dead
animal round by his tail like some kind of plaything on a
rope. She was not weeping at all, but engaged in a kind
of whooping sound as she swung the poor creature round
and round. I could not fathom her world at that moment,
and so resigned myself to preparing us a supper of leek
and potato soup. Meatless this night, to be sure.

†

'Mister Coachman?'

Her unsure tone surprised me utterly. 'Yes?'

'I— have seen the Woodmaster—'

'The— *Woodmaster* you say, Pinprick? And who
might this Woodmaster be?'

I am quite certain that my tone erupted in a truly
patronizing manner, and where normally Charlotte's
response to my insensitivity would (in the least) have
been a quick and stinging paw to my face, in this
instance she sidled close to me and wrapped her arms
about my waist with surprising constriction. 'Alright,
then,' I said. 'Tell me about him. Where did you see
him— this *Woodmaster* fellow?'

'Just above the highway, there on the eastern slope.'

'And, pray tell, *mo croi*, did he greet you?'

'He did, *mon cher*. It is how I know his name. Mister Coachman, I am terribly frightened of him and his wee people things.'

I could do nothing at this juncture but find the nearest tree stump and sit, for my legs gave way at her shocking words. *Pinprick frightened?* Utterly absurd.

'The old crone read to me about him out of her big dusty black book.'

I waited. Charlotte stood gazing into my eyes as if they were her favorite treasure. I thought I detected her tears begin to well. I put my hand out to take her to me, but she pulled away, choosing to stand in front of me, her feet placed together prim and proper.

'The old crone said he lives in the forest, but I never knew which forest, and now I know it is *this* forest, Mister Coachman!'

'Calm yourself, my love.'

'I will *not* be calm!' She then screamed bloody murder as she unsheathed her carving knife and made terrible slicing motions with it. I prayed she would not step nearer to me while engaged in such deleterious moves. My prayers were not answered as I hoped, forcing me to jump from my perch and step backwards as Charlotte approached me, her eyes glazed with hatred, or with a survivalist's terror.

'The old crone said— she read from her big book—
that he comes for children— and that after he makes
them his playthings, he *eats* them while they are yet
alive!'

'My child—' I hoped my tone would be a soothing
balm. 'Shall I go up and speak with this— this
Woodmaster?'

'No! He will slay you and roast you, Mister
Coachman! He dresses in a long red cloak and his hair is
like tongues of fire dancing round in a great wind and he
laughs like my mean Uncle Gallian! And— his wee
people things—'

'His wee *people things*, Pinprick? Pray tell, what
might these be?'

'Oh, no, Mister Coachman. *No.* I'm much too
frightened!' She replaced her weapon and ran to me,
again wrapping her arms about my waist. '*Mrum
mrumgh mruh mgrum grum.*'

'Pinprick, your words are retarded by the thickness of
my cloak.'

She lifted her mouth away from my clothing, glaring
at me. 'I said!' she replied with a huff, 'I *said*— the
Woodmaster didn't *see* me! If he had *saw* me, he would
have *ate* me. I hid behind the fairy trees.'

I didn't know how to respond. I had offered to

approach this man, or whatever he affected to be, but was halted. Charlotte was afraid for my life. This, I must say, comforted me beyond anything else which had theretofore occurred with her in our companionship. In celebration, I withdrew my pipe and packed it full of an excellent apple tobacco. In short order, smoke rings floated skyward, much to the delight of my wee charge.

'What will we do, Mister Coachman? I think my crossbow and my sword and your sword and your guns and my guns shan't hurt him at all. That is what I think.'

'Perhaps you are right, my child. Yet, may we consider, for this one instance, that you could be wrong?'

'I like it when you call me your child, Mister Coachman. Almost as much as when you call me *Pinprick.*'

'Well—'

'I said *almost.*'

†

When we arrived at the top of the eastern hill, Charlotte reached up and placed her forefinger to my lips to shush me. She then set a bolt in her crossbow. With my eyes I questioned her.

'In case of squirrels or shepherds,' she replied.

I blanched at the latter of the two prey.

'Don't worry,' she whispered. 'There is one shepherd

here promising to show me his adder. He said if I touch
its head it will spit at me, so I should be very careful. I
told him there are no serpents in Ireland. Should I see
him, for lying to me he shall be the shepherd in my
deadly aim, Mister Coachman. His time for living is
nearly finished. I hate liars.'

I was forced to bite my tongue as anger rose up in
me. My hope became that this shepherd would come
round and greet us, giving Charlotte her chance to
indeed lay him to his rest. And then was I humbled by
the altogether wider understanding that something is
horribly amiss with mankind at the outset, and, because
of this truth, there is none of us who can sit as judge over
another— for history shows us that thought proves as
poisonous as action, and so we are all guilty of
waywardness against true freedom. Being this as it may,
no tyrant, petty or otherwise, ever outlives his
punishment due him. *His spitting adder indeed!*

'Mister Coachman?'

'Yes, dear heart?'

'Put one of the apples on your head and let me shoot
it in twain.'

'I shall do no such thing!'

'*Mister-coachman-you-will-if-you-really-love-me-
mister-coachman!*'

What could I say to this? My immediate need was to

in some way divert her; cause her to become interested
in something else in the stead of my imminent death.

'Our efforts this day, Pinprick, are to attract the
Woodmaster, are they not?'

'Aye, they are. Now, take an apple from your bag,
balance it upon your noggin, and stand in front of that
oak tree just there.'

'Pinprick! You will not aim that infernal weapon at
an apple atop my head!'

'I *will* do or you shall be sorry, Mister Coachman!
Take out an apple!'

'I will not!'

The crossbow bolt penetrated my sleeve, grazing my
arm but slightly, and found its mark in a dead branch.
When I overcame my shock, I, to the surprise of the both
of us, wrenched the weapon from Charlotte's hands and
flung it over the precipice near us and down into the
trees betwixt our path and the winding mountain trail
below us.

'*Ahhhh!* My crossbow!'

'You may retrieve it later.'

'But I want it now!'

'You cannot *have* it now.'

'*Hrumph!*' And over the side of the hill she went,
through scratching limb and stinging undergrowth. Thus
ended for that day our foray in search of the red-clad

Woodmaster and his 'wee people things.'

†

Mystified was I completely by Charlotte's choice of *décor* for our cottage.

A skull, and bones.

'*We are pirates!*' There was a screech in her voice not unlike her favorite bird the *badhbh*, or carrion crow. 'Why did you put *flowers* in his eyeholes? *That looks stupid!*'

'We are most certainly *not* pirates, Pinprick. We are laudable highwaymen.'

She gave pause to my words, and then proceeded to discard my wildflowers and rearrange the animal bones round the human skull she had placed to serve as a dinner table centerpiece.

'I can think of so many more beauteous things with which to decorate the tabletop. I will not have this abominable symbolism invade my home, young lady. Remove them immediately.'

'You *will* have it, Mister Coachman! Remove *yourself* immediately!' She approached me with what appeared to be a carved twig, waving it in a tight circle as she walked. I suddenly felt weakened, as if I had not eaten for a day or more.

My vision clouding, I cried 'Pinprick! Put that infernal wand away!'

'No! The voices tell me what to do! Not you! I only do what *they* tell me!'

'The— voices?' I had heard of this sort of mental derangement. Truly, I had hoped that, with all of her murdering capability, she was not that far gone from us, but perhaps it was only my own self-delusion. No child of nine years who kills for the pure enjoyment of it can be at all sane.

'Yes. The voices.' She slipped her magic wand back into a leather holster at her side.

'Taken up witchcraft, have you?'

'It goes well with my bolts and blades.'

'Ah, I see. A witch-warrior, is it?

'Precisely.'

'Now Pinprick, these voices— are they attached to— people?' I sat at the hearth and patted an old leather ottoman, hoping she would join me. She did.

'No, they are only voices. They say bad things sometimes, and sometimes they say things that make me happy. I am happy when they tell me to kill something. I am sad when they say it is time to sleep. I don't like to sleep, because then the Woodmaster and his wee people things come in my dreams and scare me. I have seen them on the hill, but they come and scare me when I sleep as well, Mister Coachman.'

I pulled her close to me, and in one of those rare

moments with her, she lay her head on my breast, closing her eyes and breathing with ease.

'Pinprick?'

'Yes, Mister Coachman?'

'Do— you believe you might allow *my* voice to join your other friends?' I felt her body tense, but she did not open her eyes or pull away from me. 'Pinprick? What say you? May I come in and meet your friends?'

'Aye. You may, Mister Coachman. But be careful. I think they shall not like you much at all.'

'Oh, but I have a secret. Promise you shan't tell?'

'I promise. Pray tell me—'

'I will be a ghost. Then they cannot see me. How does that strike you?'

'I *like* that idea, Mister Coachman. I like it very much. I hope you frighten them silly! *Ha!*'

†

The following dusk Charlotte and I traveled from the western slope and our nestled cottage back up to the apex of the eastern slope, she and I both again intent upon ferreting out the so-called Woodmaster and his imps. I strictly forbade her to bring weapons of any kind, and was secretly exultant that she disobeyed me and ventured forth 'armed to the teeth,' as goes the piratical figure of speech.

Charlotte tugged on my sleeve. 'What if we meet the

lying shepherd as we traipse along? May I place a bolt so near his heart that at first he believes sweet Cupid to have given him visit? Or mayhap the Gopala?'

My Lord, thought I. *This child is some kind of literary savant!*

'I have, my sweet girl, dealt with the lying shepherd, as you refer to him.'

'But I wanted to kill him!'

'Oh dear heart.' I saw that it was then or never that my voice seek to intermingle with the others compelling her to do their foul bidding. In short order I found myself lifting Charlotte into the air and holding her close to me as one would a far smaller child. She acquiesced and lay her head upon my shoulder as I spoke to her. 'I met the shepherd several days ago as I took my usual morning constitutional. It was his mongrel who first discovered me, but my hasty reach to the earth for an imaginary stone set the rascal on his heels long enough for the lad to call him off.'

'*Mm-hmm*—' Charlotte nestled closer to me, taking my hair in her fingers and gently twirling it round as if it were the most fragile of golden thread.

'I then told him forthright that should he ever again mention his spitting snake to you, that I would be forced to become as our Lord and Savior and crush said serpent's head beneath my boot heel.'

'Oh! I *knew* Saint Patrick was a good man! He was
but following Jesus when he cast the nasty serpents from
Ireland, wasn't he, Mister Coachman?'

I did not mention to Charlotte that the heinous swain
at first sought to give me grief, stepping toward me with
his stave to strike me down whilst crying 'Ya damned
highwayman! I'll have yer head *and* the bounty lain on
ye!' Nor did I tell her that I sidestepped him and gave his
arm such a twist that his ligaments did crack. I then
concluded my remonstrance by giving the young man
such a sound beating about the head and neck that he
cried aloud. I am not sure that his tears revealed his
shame, his sorrow, or his anger at being caught in such
an egregious situation; but I do know, by the look in his
eyes, that as I engaged him, he stood as frightened of my
swagger as is a mouse of a housecat. It was my prayer as
I wrestled with him that I did drive the Devil from him
entirely. Neither I nor Charlotte ever saw whit of the lad
again. Good, that. She would have lain him in an early
grave. Him *and* his spitting serpent.

†

Charlotte fell fast asleep upon my shoulder, therefore
I was given the arduous task of making our way back
down the steep hill to the highway below, and then to
our cottage deep into the wood atop the western slope.
She was somewhat slight of build, nevertheless the half-

mile trundle with her attached as a dead load proved
enough to lay me down in exhaustion. I slept the night
through, though it was early evening yet when I arrived
home with my precious cargo.

†

Dawn came arduous and unrelenting in the form of
Charlotte racing into the house covered in blood and
screaming like a dying rabbit.

'Pinprick!' cried I. 'Where are you hurt? Tell me!
Where!'

'Nowhere! *Nowhere!* I *got* him, Mister Coachman! *I
shot the Woodmaster!* And look! I have one of his wee
people things!' With that she reached into the large
pocket on her cloak and pulled out what could only be
called a pocket-sized man. He was dead, one of her bolts
having split his breast into two neat portions.

'But, whence all this blood, my girl? You are
covered in it! Moreover, I thought you frightened of the
Woodmaster and his wee people.'

'I *was* frightened. I *told* you so! But this morning I
heard your voice-ghost in my head, and you said go up
and find the Woodmaster and slay him outright. So I did.
Well, not fully. He is yet alive, I believe. In truth, I can't
be sure one *can* kill him, he is so like a ghost himself.
But I slew one of his children. See?'

She held the small man up by his leg. Upside down

now, blood poured from his open mouth. I stood horrified, wanting to take the creature for a closer examination, but finding myself so abhorred by the scene that my mind whirred.

'I said— I mean my ghost-voice said nothing of the sort to you, Pinprick,' I finally managed as I, stumbling backward, found one of our wooden kitchen chairs and relaxed on it.

'It was your voice! It *was!*'

'No, it was not. I know when I speak and when I do not.'

'You are making me angry, Mister Coachman!' Charlotte dropped the Woodmaster's imp to the oval carpet and drew her short-sword, her eyes blazing like two burning coals. The current situation bade me to agree that, after all, it had been me who had instructed her to kill the Woodmaster. It was either lie to her or lie in my grave. The first lie proved the happier of the two.

4

Orange

Next night came, a lightless night— and though I persisted against her, Charlotte insisted that this was the night, 'the perfect night,' to confront the Woodmaster. My resolution was to placate her, and hope that she would not again drift away to sleep before the necessary encounter. I will admit that on this occasion I felt even more of a trepidation than I had the previous times we ventured out for confrontation. Yet why would I not feel apprehension? Not only had I witnessed with mine own eyes a creature, if diminutive, so foul as to surely have been the product of the darkest sorcery, I also strode forth to confront an unknown and presumably malign spirit with a child who had somehow contracted with the Devil himself. I did not find this current predicament extremely hopeful.

†

'Mister Coachman?'

'Yes?'

'I can smell him. Here, you hold the lantern.'

At that moment a not altogether unpleasant waft of burning oak assailed my nostrils. For whatever reason, it was just then that I noticed Charlotte's attire.

'What, pray tell, have you tied to your pants legs?'

'Bloody squirrel intestines.'

As per usual with Charlotte's antics, my own blood rushed from my face. As my sight dimmed, I was required to befriend a giant beech, and the majestic power of my new ally renewed me with a quickness which I can only consider miraculous.

'Pinprick! What— *why?*'

'The old crone told me to do it should I ever be in peril of my life against something ungodly.'

The 'old crone.' Charlotte had mentioned her several times. Could this have been her Nanny Mathers? It was then I noticed the black feathers tied into her hair, the Red Indian face-paint, and the string of crow skulls dangling behind her like some kind of morbid animal tail.

'Pinprick!'

'Yes, Mister Coachman?'

'You are utterly terrifying!'

'Oh, *thank* you, Mister Coachman!'

†

In my life, I had known sure terror. The meeting of Charlotte Proorice had grayed me considerably, and only within the first fortnight of our acquaintance. Yet, this *Night of the Woodmaster*, as I shall call it, did something to me which I am not sure I can relate in proper philosophical terms. Notwithstanding, I must needs tell what occurred, or what I *believe* to have occurred, and therefore let my readers decide to their own satisfaction.

Bird skulls clacking behind her and feathers whipping this way and that in her long wavy hair, Charlotte, staying well within the light afforded by our one lantern, hummed an olden tune that every so often I thought I knew, but not enough to make the proper connection and join in chorus. The squirrel innards tied round her knees were giving up quite a stink already, but I dared not mention this to her for fear that on this darksome, treacherous path one of her childish outbursts would have the effect of darkening my sight forever. She was, after all, again 'armed to the teeth,' so to speak. A rapier, a brace of pistols, a dirk, a sword sheathed to her back, and crossbow with full quiver and nimble finger. Nothing except something undeniably supernatural would be able to withstand this wee demon I had grown to love so dearly.

'Hark! I hear something!' Charlotte threw herself to the ground. 'Get down!'

I jumped, suddenly crawling with invisible vermin. 'Charlotte! You quite frightened me out of my skin!'

'*Grrrrr!* Mister Coachman! You have called me *Charlotte* again, and I do not like *Charlotte*! *I hate Charlotte*! And I forbid you to ever call me *Charlotte* ever, ever again!'

But this was not, of course, the end to her diatribe. Verbal retribution, as I knew quite well already, was almost always accompanied with something sharp aimed at my throat, my eyes, my midsection, my knees, or somesuch other tender portion of my person. This incident proved no different. Before I had time to set up defense with my stave— perhaps knock whatever weapon she had in mind from her hands, or perhaps even knock *her* to the ground— that familiar icy burn invaded my being, and blood gushed forth from a wound at my left rib cage.

'Pinprick! What— what have you done? You've *cut* me!'

'Oh pish-posh! It is only a flesh wound, Mister Coachman. You fret about such preposterous things. Wrap your scarf about yourself and hold the lantern up so I can see through the dark. It shall soon be time for the Woodmaster to arrive.'

I did as I was told. What else was I to do? The child had me, heart and soul. She could murder me with thousands of knives, and I believe I would have died smiling, my love for her was so all-consuming. I worshipped the child.

'*There once was a man from Kilkennyyy!*' sang Charlotte. '*Who thought he would never get anyyy!*'

This song, I had learned, always accompanied her as

she made water. This necessity she carried out nearly as expediently as any lad could have, and was soon back at my side as we trekked along the sheep trail which, at a certain turn not many miles ahead, led unto a wider path through the Wicklow Mountains. Oh, aye. I had thought it a fine plan to soon go in farming disguise and follow that highway. A man often requires more than one way in his life to follow, and a glen of no more than a mile long and a furlong wide, from peak to peak, was bound, because of Charlotte's antics, to be soon overrun in the name of righteous indignation.

†

Before us, and from nowhere, stood a fiery man much as Pinprick had briefly described, his longish ginger hair blowing in a breeze which was not with the girl and me, thus proving itself to be an infernal wind of Hell. The Woodmaster spoke to us, his vivid green eyes wide with hateful amusement, yet it was as if I had lost all of my ability to hear.

'Pinprick,' I said as she suddenly misplaced all of her gallantry and cowered like a frightened kitten at my feet, her face hidden in the folds of my cloak as if behind the most unrevealing mask. 'Pinprick, can you hear the man? For I cannot.'

A sudden rush of scorching air, accompanied by a blazing light as if from an exploded round, caused me to uplift my precious charge and run for shelter behind the nearest beech, thankfully one of large enough size that it could have hidden five grown men from full sight of the enemy, had it needed to engage itself in that happy manner.

'Come out!' cried a low and menacing voice. 'Who, pray tell, have ye brought with ye, me wee love?'

Charlotte did not reply. I would not have expected her to reply, seeing that she had fainted dead away, lying crumpled at my knee, her mouth opened wide as if frozen in a scream. Her eyes, thankfully, were closed, or I may have thought her already taken up by the Valkyries.

'Pinprick,' I whispered. 'Wake up, *mo croi! Mo croi!*'

She did not awaken, and so I lay her head upon the lichen-covered root of the tree, summoned my inner strength with a breath and a prayer, and stood. I felt no further heat on the air, and so, terrified but knowing something must be done, I stepped from behind our natural shelter into the unholy glow to countenance the miscreant.

'*Ha!* Ye have bollocks after all, I see!' bellowed the red-cloaked man, this so-called Woodmaster. 'I will make our parley as brief as possible, sirrah! Thy wee bitch there, hidden ahind thy salvific tree, has slain one o' me lads. Now, the recompense be a simple one. Might ye guess?'

'You'll not harm the child!' I replied, my words feeling like clean water shooting forth from the mountainside.

'Oh, I'll *harm* her alright, sirrah! One o' my lads lay dead, *she* slew him like some kind of bloody savage with her goddamned crossbow, and I *will* have her head in his stead! *After* I tie her up and use her as my bauble for a time. Are we understood? Or shall I again rearrange the wind and fry ye to a crisp this very moment?'

How I spoke again, I do not know. In the same manner that I held my loosened bowels, I suppose. *Miraculously.*

'I am the highwayman John Coppe! My charge is none other than Charlotte Proorice of Dublin's Proorice House! We regulate this acre, sirrah! Hence, your money, or your life!'

With that I stepped toward the demon as I would any potential customer of my savvy, my rapier drawn, my eyes piercing his very soul. This, thought I, would be a tremendous battle of will, yet my trump lay in that he defended ghoulish creatures the height of new saplings (which I believe he must have created as thralls to his satanic will), and my sole reason for existence had become a wee twist of a girl whom I loved as if she were my own offspring.

'Well, John Coppe the highwayman! Come nearer and know my wrath! If, naturally, ye have the necessary stones! I've not lain eyes upon a cur as ugly as ye since after I kicked my mother to death afore I left home.'

'Belay that profane talk!' cried I to the scoundrel, be he unearthly or no. Soon after, we engaged in hand-to-hand combat, he with orbs of fire he called forth and I with my sword, which I, not being lightly skilled, in a turn of fortune ran through the very heart of this purported *Woodmaster*, to discover that his sorcery, however Luciferian, proved unable to save his fully human form from an inability to further house his eternal soul.

My God. I had slain my first man. I fell, weeping like a cataract after a storm and praying that he would be my last. As I knelt upon the dewy earth, a multitude of his naked imps swarmed from every crevice of the shadowy forest and gathered about their fallen Woodmaster as coastal villagers will gather, awestruck, about a beached leviathan. And then there rose up such a keening for the dead man that I stood and backed away for fear the demons would turn their sorrow upon me in a fit of rage. My worst fear was indeed realized, for one, then three, then five, then at least a score gathered as one force and stalked toward me, intending, I assumed, to

pull me to the ground and consume me outright. But Charlotte's bolts were soon on the fly. One, then three, then five, then a score and more were lain to rest by her missile and my blade. I will admit here that I held no remorse for chopping the rancid gargoyles to pieces where they stood! I do not believe them to have been in the least bit capable of contrition or change of heart.

Charlotte then ran to the dead man and with her dagger performed a certain act upon him which shall not here be detailed. 'That's so he can't tie any girls up in Hell and do mean things to them. Like he told me he would do to me when he caught me.'

✝

'Pinprick! I strictly forbid your decorating our home with the heads of those ungodly creatures! *They have begun to stink!*'

'I shall do as I please, Mister Coachman! *Ha! Your* head would look nice as a new centerpiece for the table! Stretch your neck out! *Stretch it out!*'

'*Ach!* Pinprick! How can you *speak* to me in such a disrespectful manner?'

She lowered her eyes. 'It wasn't me. It was Orange.'

I took pause. *Orange?* The voices. Of course. She was haunted with disembodied voices as would be an old house awash in fright and bloodshed. Poor, sweet Charlotte.

'This— *Orange*. He doesn't seem very friendly, Pinprick. A good mate of yours, is he?'

'Well— not really. He is one of the Green Shadows.'

'Are you— frightened of him?'

'Oh heavens no, Mister Coachman! *Hahahahaha!*'

'Come and sit with me. Talk with me about your— the voices. Will you? I would know more of Orange, and of these Green Shadows, did you say?'

She put the handsaw down with which she had been decapitating the several dozen bodies of the dead she had collected and swept to me as if she were the sweetest princess of a girl one could ever wish to be found in the presence of. After wiping errant gouts of blood from her fingers all over my trousers, she cupped my face in her gory hands and, aye, kissed me. I was taken aback, for she had never before placed her lips to mine, and though her daughterly action was indeed a comfort to me, it proved a new and rather bewildering experience.

'I kissed you,' she whispered, smiling.

'Yes. Yes you did, Pinprick.'

'And you kissed me.'

'I do believe that to be the case. Yes.'

'Will you be my daddy, Mister Coachman?'

I felt my eyes, welling with tears, search her own for some *real* Charlotte hidden behind the varied guises of her private demons. A warmth radiated from her face. Her eyes, indeed, now spoke of a soul clean of all selfishness. Tiny streams trickled down her bright pink cheeks, and her body quivered.

'Orange,' she reported, 'is much like the Woodmaster. Yet he is a bit more friendly. He is one of the Green Shadows. There are five of them. Orange, Hallow, Gloom, Bone-Snap, and Bloody-Tongue.'

I shivered.

'I like Orange the best,' she continued. 'Even though he is mean, he makes me laugh. And I like to laugh.'

'Will Orange talk to me? Or, will any one of the others? Would they like to speak with me?'

'I think— no. They don't know that you are the New Ghost. They are terribly, terribly frightened of you, but they don't know that *you* are that ghost. I think they would recognize your voice if I let you come in dressed as you are right now. You said you would be a ghost in my head, Mister Coachman, and you did. I am happy of that.'

'I— I am happy as well, Pinprick.'

†

Next day brought torrents of rain, and so of necessity Charlotte and I remained indoors. She desired that I read to her, and it was a fortunate thing that the last of our heroic holdups had procured for us a satchel full of

beautifully gilded volumes of poetry and fairytales, as
well as richly crafted prose for the more grown-up mind.
Fairytales were that which Charlotte wished to hear, and
so I did oblige her, also to my own fanciful delight.
Thereafter, over several pots of steaming nettle tea and
biscuits of a delightful buttery design, we read the day
away together. One particular tale, a short one indeed,
seemed to completely mesmerize Charlotte. For days
after, she pretended to be various characters from it, and
I must admit that I did admire her thespian talents, so
rich were they for such a young child. Had she been
trained in the performing arts by someone in her house?
Whatever the case, what follows is but a portion of said
fairytale as I remember it:

*As I awoke, a man sniffed at my skin and laughed. 'You
smell of fresh meat!' cried he. 'You smell as if you
expect to be eaten alive! What sort of boy would run
round in such a thick fog as this?' I could tell that the
man truly hungered for my flesh. If I did not provide him
with a sacrifice to abate his sorrow, he would eat me.
Soon, though, he fell asleep, and I ran away and far. As I
approached the top of the nearest hill, a white light
blinded me for an instant. When I could again see, I
spied a white dragon shifting over the mountain like a
layer of foam riding ocean waves. I could tell by its*

movement that it was a territorial creature; I could tell that it would fight me before allowing me to venture any further. And so I turned and ran the other way; away from the dragon, away from the flesh-eating man.

The sound of pattering steps nipped at my heels as I ran. Looking behind me, I saw a giant black wolf following me. It carried on its back a lady who wore dragon-scale armor. Her white hair trailed in the wind. Suddenly, a general dressed in black and red and wearing white paint on his face and hands and feet asked me who I was and how I came to be there. I told him about the flesh-eating man, about the white dragon, and about the colossal wolf and lady following me. His eyes opened in delight, and he drew his quill and ink to scribble my words on yellow parchment. Then, a swarm of angry carrion crows swooped upon the general and began to peck at every orifice and crevice of his body. A mass of flapping and cawing round a core of struggling flesh, they danced a violent jig. The man's pitiful screams were drowned in a sea of screeches and the nauseating sounds of countless beaks piercing his flesh. I ran from this bloody scene as quickly as I could, and straight into the arms of the lady with the white flowing hair. The wolf upon which she had been riding allowed me to get upon its back. 'I will be your guide and protector,' it whispered, 'as we seek your mother, to

55

save her from the white dragon who has captured her.'

†

I should perhaps say here that though I enjoyed very much Charlotte's reenactments of the running boy, the flesh-eating man, the white dragon, the strange and ill-fated general, the lady, and the huge wolf, I found myself disturbed by the tale as if it were one of my more horrible visions, thinking it more of a nightmare than a fairytale for children. In truth, I was sorry I had read the piece to her, thinking that perhaps I had succeeded in adding yet more voices to her head filled with enough of them already. That curséd Uther Culpeper! I vowed to never read another line of his work to Charlotte— nor even to myself! My dreams have not *yet* righted themselves for the uncanny tales of that author! (Aye, in my private time I did read more than the one—)

†

'Mister Coachman?'

'Yes, dear heart?'

'Why do you love me, Mister Coachman?'

'I simply do, my girl. I love you because you are you.'

'Don't I frighten you?'

'Aye, you do that, sure. But all girls frighten the ones who love them. It is merely the way of things.'

'Truly? All girls are frightening?'

56

'Would I lie to you, Pinprick?'

'No. Mister Coachman. You would never lie.'

5

Knights of the Road

In my mulling moments I had thought that perhaps, in time, I would become less and less shocked at the deplorable actions of Charlotte 'Pinprick' Proorice— *fille horrible.*

I enjoyed no such fortune.

A moneyed ecclesiastical stagecoach from Dublin, we discovered through a certain nefarious acquaintance, was to be traveling through *Glean na Gruagh* three days thence. Our associate, I should adjoin, was not a highwayman *per se*, and so I had good reason to trust him when he agreed not to inform the additional robbers of our glen of the clergymen's illustrious arrival. I believed his word, for Trilly Hassleby supped with us on regular occasion, being at this time of his life enfeebled and nearly incapable of procuring his own meat. A pathetic cripple of one leg, one eye, and a claw hand, he stood at great disadvantage should Charlotte, whom he was understandably terrified of, wish to stalk and slay him outright. This latter thought was never agreeable to me, but, to my chagrin, I held minimal control over my charge, though she had happily accepted my voice into her circle of invisible friends.

†

I stepped from the shadowy wood with an echoing blunderbuss shot as Charlotte, coming from the opposite side of the highway, fired her crossbow, the bolt piercing the breast of the armed guard who sat next to the driver. Tossing my gun aside, I pulled my brace of pistols and brandished them.

'Stand and deliver, sirrahs!' cried Charlotte as she swaggered forth, her newly acquired red hooded cloak billowing in the cool breeze of that frosty morn. 'Thy money, or thy life!'

'Oh, what a show!' cried a dandy of a priest as he poked his head from the coach window, his powdery white peruke in coiffure to a high degree indeed, a look of ecstatic surprise on his aged features. I reckoned he did not yet know of the death of his guard.

'And who have we here?' the clergyman continued, his eyebrows prancing with sheer delight. 'Oh, isn't she lovely, Father William! Why, it is Red Riding Hood come to greet us from her wolven wood! And she is armed, no less! Oh, tell me someone! Tell me! Who has orchestrated such a feast for our eyes this day! He who has done so deserves a fine meal and an improvement in his situation, to be sure! *Oh!*'

'Reverend de Berge, Sir!' cried the driver. 'Head down!' And those were the unfortunate man's last words, I am saddened to say. As if Charlotte were some kind of climbing animal, she scaled the side of the coach, knocked the cocked pistol from the man's grasp, and sliced him a new mouth— red and wide from ear to ear.

Gladdened that my continuous sorrow did not follow me to the decisive moment of thieving account, with a quickness I had the Reverend's two religious associates beneath my guns, demanding they drop theirs, and forthwith, to the path. Charlotte, having none of my genteel behavior on this day (or any other whilst 'on account'), slipped a dirk beneath the first priest's ribcage like a knife into butter and, quick as lightning, discharged her flintlock as its barrel lay upon the second man's temple.

'Pinprick!' was all I could straightaway cry as I stood with the poor soul's blood and brain matter covering me. 'Oh, God! Charlotte no!' I then cried, but again I was too late. The foppish Reverend de Berge was dead, half hanging from his carriage doorway, a shortsword piercing his brain through his eye sinister.

Stunned by the ethereal presence of the newly dead, yet regathering myself more quickly than I would have ever believed possible, I set two of the four horses of the ornate ecclesial carriage free to go where they so pleased. Then, with Charlotte's assist, and the aid of the two remaining animals, I stripped the coach clean of its prize consisting of gold doubloon, rich clothing, and foodstuffs galore. Charlotte held a particular liking for mincemeat. It was apparent that the priest and his mates had enjoyed that delicacy as well.

It was then that a most infandous thing occurred; an event which yet sends chills of horror to the very depth of my spirit.

'Would you be ready for the traipse home, Pinprick?' I asked as I made the last hemp knot secure for our travel unto the steep western woodland hill, and thus back to our cottage nestled there.

I received no answer from her, but instead heard a slurping, burbling sound. Fox-like, I moved round the coach. The scene greeting me was one which must be common on the battlefields of Hell. There, kneeling over the driver, was Charlotte. Cupped in her hands she held something large and purplish—

In her single-minded euphoria she must have heard me approach, for she looked up at me and growled like a rabid dog— her eyes wide with a glee which spoke of delight and of evil combined— a gangrenous merriment which ate her alive yet concurrently nurtured her with its insistence that she do as she please, when she please, as long as she please. Her beautiful alabaster features, her rosy cheeks, her white lace collar, the front of her cloak— all spattered with freshly spilled blood.

'Want some, Mister Coachman?'

I did not reply. I *could* not.

Drawing my sword, I walked toward her in a flash of madness, intent upon dispatching this beast, this angel, whom I loved as my own soul.

'Stay thine hand, sir!'

I whirled.

'Stay thine hand, I say!'

Before us stood five stalwart men, four of them dressed as 'knights of the road.' The speaker stepped forward, two pistols cocked and leveled at me. 'Unhand thy rapier, sir.'

I did as I was told.

'John Coppe!' barked the speaker. 'Master Coppe, look closely in thy newfound delirium. I do reckon ye shall know us all soon enough.'

Again, I did as commanded. I gazed upon each face, and, aye, I knew the men. They were representatives of the clans of the two fellow cutthroats Charlotte slew when we first entered the glen as potential victims to that which, as the will of God would have it, soon became our own trade, as it were.

'Are you here to turn on your word?' I begged. 'To at last take revenge for your lost kin? If so, there could not be a finer day, for I am like a lovelorn maiden, deeply wounded of soul in this time, and so very much do long to have an end to it all. I beg of ye, then. Take my life. *Take it now!*'

I turned and sprang for my rapier, fully intending to aggravate one or more of the gentlemen into slaying me with speed— but this was not the end result of my rashness. Rather, the speaker, who I recognized to be none other than Jacob Copper, brother of the murdered John Copper, pulled the trigger of his pistol, lodging a ball in the brain of the guard upon which Charlotte was feasting. The man *groaned!* and released his death rattle! Oh my Lord, the horror! The poor creature had not yet died as that child of a demon had begun eating his heart! I fell to my knees, no longer having the strength for suicide.

'Harry,' spoke Jacob Copper. 'Take the girl up, by her wrists, and bring her away from that.'

A whiskery man of middle age strode to Charlotte in a fearless gait, took her arms, gazed with tenderness upon her, and then drew her into his bosom. She pushed her face into the crevice of his neck as he walked back to his lads. I surmised this man to be the infamous robber Headless Harry.

'Will ye be sharing thy bounty with us then, Master Coppe?' came Jacob's rhetorical question.

I nodded, sore of heart. 'Take all of it, if you will. I care not.'

'Fair be fair, Coppe,' added Tommy Pockets, who dressed more as a shepherd than a 'knight' or nobleman. 'We'll take but half of the bounty. After all, thy girl has brought a swift close to the necessaries. And to that, ye, sir, be renowned for being bloodless. Thy peaceable hand, like all Ireland's hero Cu Ruí, be duly admired amongst us.'

'Divide the findings, then, if thou will, Mousy,' spoke Jacob to a third one of their company as he drew in a virile breath. 'Leave the greater portion of victuals for the child and her master. Mr. Twiddle, sir. Will thou be so kind as to join Mousy in his task?'

'Aye, Jacob. Happy to, sir. What say, Mousy? A pocket full o' rye, hey boyo?'

'I shall leave the libation to ye, Iva Twiddle. Thou art much better at the drink than I— me mother being Red Indian.'

At this strange confession I started. How had Mousy come then to be an Irish highwayman?

Headless Harry let Charlotte down then, and with no further ado, taking what they would of our prize, yet, true to their word, only half of the goods, the five men receded, laughing like Robin and his Merry Men, into the woodland, and were again surreptitious in their wanderings.

Later that night, once Charlotte was dead to the

world, I returned and buried the bodies by lanternlight. For all others entering our dark abode after that day, five hastily fashioned crosses planted in the earth would prove as much a deterrent, though softer on the eye, than the same number of corpses.

†

Several days elapsed before I could speak again. Charlotte sought to converse with me throughout the first day, but upon discovering me incoherent, sought other diversions which led to an entirely novel *décor* of wildflowers, bloodstones, pastel draperies suspended from iron hooks hammered in the wall crevices, and knives of all shapes and origins. Oh, aye. There remained also the usual skulls, including the human head she had found and thought it 'perfectly piratey.' Yet, and for a reason unbeknownst to me given her complete selfishness in matters concerning her world, she removed the decapitated heads of the wee dead men (who had been magically fashioned by the deceased Woodmaster). For this was I grateful, but feared not tell her so lest she feel the need to bring them back, or perhaps something worse, in order to continue receiving attention from me along those dark lines. Neglected children are like that. Compliments for good actions are read by them as ends to the attention given, and so the preference for them is war, not peace— for in war they

are being heard, being paid attention to. And also, with
Pinprick there were the additional voices, a difficulty
even the most neglected child by and large never
encounters.

†

'Pinprick?'

'Mister Coachman! You've come home!'

I smiled, and agreed with a nod. 'Come,' I beckoned,
and as she did, I moved my Bible away and took her into
my lap.

'Wait! I want to put more turf on the fire!' So she did
that, but was soon back with me. 'Talk to me, Mister
Coachman. Tell me a story, or simply talk. You've been
speechless for *days*. I've missed you *terribly*.'

'Right, then. Well, what would you like to discuss?'

'*Um*— Well, I can tell you more about the Green
Shadows. Nay, I might even like to *introduce* you.
Would you like that, Mister Coachman?'

'Oh, aye! Your mates Orange, Hallow, Gloom, Bone-
Snap, and Bloody-Tongue. Would I be correct then?'

'Oh Mister Coachman! You *remember* them!'

Charlotte hugged me then, and kissed my cheek
before she leaned back to look me squarely in the face.
'Orange leads the rest, much as Jacob Copper leads *his*
men. Now, since you have been gone away from me this
half week, Gloom has come to me, to tell me he is very,

66

very frightened. *Much* more frightened than the others.'
And then her voice changed, growing deep and raspy as
the pupils of her eyes grew large.

'I am panicky!' whined Gloom. 'There is a ghost in
here, in this house! Out, foul ghost! *Out!*'

'There is no ghost!' rebuked Orange; and I knew it
must be Orange, for it was the same fierce, defiant voice
Charlotte used when she challenged me.

'There *is* a ghost,' came a reply in a tone which
sounded as if it might be Charlotte when she was much
smaller. 'And it scares me.'

'Who is speaking now?' I asked, already nearing
bewilderment.

'I hear the ghost again!' cried Gloom. 'Make it go
away! Go away, you horrid ghost! *Go away!*'

I knew that if I paid more attention to Gloom, I
would lose the wee girl's voice which now acutely
intrigued me. 'Child?' I said. 'Please don't go away.
What is your name?'

'I am— Hallow. Do you like my dolly?'

Charlotte took from the folds of her long white shirt a
thing which I saw immediately to be the desiccated
corpse of a goat kid newly born. Where she had gotten
the gruesome thing, to make use of it as a doll, I could
not fathom. I knew that farmers often buried stillborns
deep in their haystacks. Had Charlotte been digging

67

round in one of them, only to discover the morbid creature and think it a plaything?

'Hello, Hallow,' I replied through my revulsion. 'You are very pretty. And aye, I *do* like your doll. What is her name?'

'Her name is Charlotte. She is dead, but I still love her. Would you like to hold her?'

'Well,' I said. 'Aye. Let me hold her.' I took the vile thing in trembling hands. 'You both are very pretty.'

'Cradle her, please. She will cry if you don't.'

I cradled the morbidity.

'Hallow thanks ye kindly, sirrah! And wilt be gladdened when ye die! *Harrr!*'

A chill shot through me like a brisk wintry wind. Now, who was this? I gathered my courage to ask, and was not surprised with the reply.

'I be Bloody-Tongue, sirrah! Now shut thine hole afore I cram it full o' me sausage!'

'*Ach!* Hush! He needn't shut *anything*, Bloody-Tongue. Thou forget thy place! Please pardon me mate, Mr. Coppe. A bit lazy and loud he be. We keep him about for his rakishness alone, otherwise we would dispense of him, and properly, I assure thee. Me name be Bone-Snap. Pleased to meet thee, as be we all.'

'I be not pleased!' replied Bloody-Tongue.

'Silence, dog!' shouted Orange. 'Pinprick, you may

speak if you like.'

'I will then,' replied Charlotte, and her eyes straightaway became normal to look into. Her face relaxed back to its sweet demeanor— for as each voice spoke, her countenance took on a comparable fixture. For Orange, she became cold and manipulative. I was, as I have said, very familiar with Orange. Gloom caused her face to screw up as if she were in pain, or found in great fear for her life— or her sanity. Bloody-Tongue caused Charlotte's countenance to become roguish, the corners of her mouth curved into an evil sneer, her eyes snapping with pure hatred. Bone-Snap was authoritative like Orange, but more subdued and, when he spoke, her features, though yet only of nine years, became much like that of a hardened miner or fisherman. I do believe Hallow to have been Charlotte when she was but three, or perhaps four at the most— a true babe in the wood. With it all, however, I found each voice, in its own way, truly revolting. And why? They were not my Charlotte, but parts of her, or not parts of her at all. Shards of her, or shards of her terrible experiences inside that mansion in Rathmines, or unclean spirits come to make their abode in a helpless child. What terrible things had she been forced to live through in that house? I was not sure I wanted to know. What I *was* sure of was that I, or my voice, was haunting the very spirits haunting her, and

this knowledge filled me with such a feeling of
merriment that I could hardly contain my laughter. But I
did so, for the child's sake. Charlotte would want to
know why I was laughing, and so my joy may have had
a diverse effect upon her as she sat open, her demons on
full display. In truth, I knew not what *else* she had
hidden in the folds of her shirt.

†

Would my nightmare not find its end? Next day at
dawn we were visited by the cripple Trilly Hassleby, and
before he could finish his breakfast and tell us his newest
tale, Charlotte had poisoned him to death with a mug of
foxglove tea. Upon my begging her, and with copious
tears, as to why she had murdered our valuable friend,
she would only answer that it had been he to bring down
Jacob Copper and his gang upon us that day, and if they
had not come, we would be double the richer for our
work with the Reverend and his priestly companions.
I could say nothing to soothe her, and so, nothing more
to it, I spent the better part of that morning searching for
a suitable place to bury Master Hassleby. As I patted his
clothing for jewelry, money, or other things of potential
value, I came across a paper sealed with a red waxen
stamp. I went cold where I knelt, not sure whether I
should break the seal or bury the letter with our friend.
Then, coming to my senses, I broke the letter open and

read, as follows:

I, Reverend Gerard de Berge, do hereby, with full power given me by Her Majesty Anne Stewart, grant full clemency to one, John Malachi Coppe, of Stoneybatter, Dublin, heretofore outlawed for the crimes of kidnapping, evasion of law, thievery, and murder. My reasons for the clemency of this man have been made clear before my peers, and there are more to stand with me on this matter than against me. Mr. Coppe, it appears, has become the unwilling servant of Proorice House, an ungodly establishment which shall remain in mine eye criminal and ever worthy of the harshest judgments. Therefore, let this letter, and the three others written in copy like it, one of which shall forever be on public record, be carried by Mr. Coppe until such time as he is well known to be freed of his accusers and steps forth as a free man once again.

*Signed and sealed this day in the
Year of Our Lord, July 13, 1707,
the Reverend Gerard de Berge,
the Church of England,
in the Name of Her Majesty Anne Stewart,
Queen of Great Britain and Ireland*

✝

I feel sure that my ache of heart at this discovery can be fully understood. Of course I did not relate a word of my knowledge to Charlotte. What would have been my reason?

The kind and insightful man wishing to grant me full clemency was dead, and Pinprick had killed him.

✝

I awoke to a particularly strong scent of burning turf. Jumping from my bed, I stumbled into the main room to find Charlotte sitting in the middle of the floor next to a stack of smoking peat.

'Charlotte! What are you doing?'

'You are making me angry, Mister Coachman. You know my name. It is Pinprick. That is all it is. That is all it ever shall be.'

'You'll set the rug to fire!'

'It's a burning castle. A warlord came and said he wanted the land, and so now all the lords and ladies are dead, and their castle burns. Do you like my story?'

As best I could, I tossed the hot bricks, one by one, into the hearth. I met no resistance. Charlotte merely sat there and watched me work. Afterward, as if nothing at all had happened, she boiled a kettle of freshly drawn spring water and made us hot muesli, loaded with currants, for breakfast.

'Tell me a story, Mister Coachman. I told you my

story, now you must tell me one.'

'I have a better idea. I am very hungry for stories this morning, so I would like for you to tell me another. Would you do that for me?'

'I reckon, aye. Get comfortable, then, for it may be strange.'

'One small thing, though. What is that you have wrapped round your wrist, Pinprick?'

'That dead priest's collar. I thought it made a nice bracelet.'

'Oh I see.' I could say nothing else of value to the situation. Putting my empty bowl on the floor, I shifted in my chair as if to say that I was ready for her tale. She began.

Once upon a time, I saw my father fall, and then the ground swallowed him alive. I knew that he was gone forever. 'Tell me what it is you have come here seeking,' three shepherds said to me. Their voices sounded like they were growling. I did not like them at all. 'I can go anywhere I want to with a turn of this silver ring,' I replied to them. They smelled my skin. 'You smell like fresh meat,' they said. 'You smell like you expect to be eaten alive. What kind of girl would run round in fog like this?' Under my feet I felt music playing, and so I began to dance. The three shepherds laughed at me. Then I thought maybe it was them making the music. My toes began to burn, and I didn't wish to dance anymore, but yet, I could not stop. 'Stop!' I screamed at my feet, but they would not stop. While I danced, I prayed for something to come and fill up the sad part of me not understanding anything about this world. I tried to turn my silver ring, but reckoned that the old woman who gave it to me had lied to me, for I did not vanish as she said I would. 'Let me go!' I yelled. Then I began to cry. The mean shepherds laughed at me even harder. 'Look how she dances! She dances like some crazy fisherman!' Then a woman with pretty eyes appeared before us. She looked much like a girl I had seen before, but she was older, and instead of crow black hair she had white hair like snow, and she stood on one foot. 'You there, come here,' the woman said. 'Dancing girl. I can help you, dancing girl.' I shied away from her. The shepherds stopped laughing and merely looked at both of us. Their faces were like blank pieces of parchment. 'Who are you?' asked one of the shepherds to the strange woman. 'I am called by many names,' the lady replied. 'Badhbh, Blaithnait, Brigid, Banba, Samhain, Etain, Cailleach, Nemhain, Macha, Morrigan, Maeve, Macalla, Ana, Annis, Anu, Dergu, Deirdre, Danu.' They marveled at her. 'Names with

nothing to spare, them,' said another of the
shepherds as they all three backed away from her.
Suddenly I stopped dancing, and I was so happy I
began to weep. And that is the end of my story. The
end.

†

That night I awoke in sweats several times. And old woman stood facing me, her bright blue eyes shining as she said to me, over and again, 'Be Christ in this world, good sir. Thus be your life's work, and nothing beside. Be Christ in this world, milord.'

†

An evening stroll along a lesser used path in the glen was a customary activity of mine. At times I would find Charlotte trying to make squirrels talk to her. In these moments I would leave her to her imagination, with a prayer for the wee creature as I continued on my way. On one particular late afternoon, though, I heard a chorus of children playing, and as I stood so as to get a clearer impression of the voices, I distinctly made out Charlotte's voice from amongst the others, and was suddenly horror-struck. Where were they playing? *What* were they playing? The other children simply did not understand the great danger they were in! I had to find them before disaster came upon them at Charlotte's hand! And so I ran upward toward the apex of the eastern hill, sensing this would be where I would find them among the giant oak trees growing there time out of mind.

The summit of the glen and I met one another, yet there were no children to be seen, and their voices had stilled. To and fro I ran. No children. Had I heard the fairyfolk? No, I told myself. I had been aware of Charlotte's voice. I had indeed heard Charlotte's voice.

I needed rest. I was losing my sanity. Living with this wee terror was taking its toll on me, and I knew that if I did not take immediate action, I was in danger of losing all capacity to operate properly in the world I had come to know.

The solution— the cure, if you will— came from a surprising source. I *say* cure. Perhaps I mean respite of a kind, though not a kind I would ever advise.

6

On Holiday in Hell

'I want to see the ocean, Mister Coachman. Will you please take me there?'

I needed no more words to know that it was precisely this— a trip to the shore— that I required for my health and wellbeing. Nay, perhaps even my very salvation. The part of Bay Bretesche I thought would be most beautiful lay but a half day's ride from our home in *Gleann na Gruagh*. I knew the place well, and upon inquiry, found that Bone-Snap also knew it, and missed it dearly.

†

'Mister Coachman! Hurry! We should be leaving! It is nigh noon-o'-night!'

'Hold your horses, young lady. Can you not see that I am packing our necessary provisions? A helping hand from you would give the Devil less fingers.'

'Ha! That was *funny*, Mister Coachman! Would my helping feet give him less toes?'

'I might say they would, Pinprick, if he *had* toes, that is.'

'Poor Satan! He has no toes? How does he walk then?'

'He has hooves, or so it is said.'

'So he walks on his hind legs because they're horse legs?'

'Goat legs.'

'Ach! *Goat* legs! Mister Coachman! Surely you jest!'

'Not according to the books I've read about him.'

'The Devil has his own Bible?'

'Well— no, Pinprick. Or perhaps—'

'Which is it then! You are making me angry, Mister Coachman! And you know what happens when I get angry! I walk on *my* hind legs!'

I backed away to a safe distance from Charlotte. 'That you do, and I am sorry I have in some way upset you. Might we speak on another subject?'

'Only if you promise me to tell me more about the Devil one day not long from now. I want to know everything that you know about him.'

'I make you the promise that I will tell you all that I know. For now, though, may we not consider our holiday soon to be undertaken?'

She answered me by running outside to the stable, where I heard her talking to our horses, now four in all.

'It shall be you two who'll take us, for you are the quickest, and it's a grand thing as well that you are both black as night.'

I was not prepared for what next I heard.

'Pinprick,' a strange voice said. 'I, too, would like to

travel to Bay Bretesche.'

'You are as bright as a full moon, white horse,' replied Charlotte. 'People can see you from miles away. No, you are only good for carrying supplies in the daytime. Sorry.'

'What about me?' asked the other horse (I assumed— a deeper tenor than the first). 'I am red as Gypsy blood. I am hard to see in the night, and I, too, love the Irish Sea.'

'You may carry our tent and supplies, red horse. We shall ride the black horses. It is settled.'

'But what about the daytime,' the white horse came again. 'White is harder seen in the sunshine.'

A brief silence came as Charlotte gave pause to the horse's words.

'What you say may indeed be true, white horse,' she then said, 'but I have decided. Please eat your oats and be quiet now.'

A hour later we were well on our way south to Bay Bretesche, and, our journey being happily uneventful, by dawn we arrived and made camp near the Anglo-Norman motte (once sporting a brattice, or 'British,' and giving this bay its historical place-name).

†

'Pinprick, love. Why have you splayed your hair out at such odd angles?'

'I am a witch, remember—'

'Oh, aye. So you are. I had forgotten. Might Pinprick the Witch like to share biscuits and tea with her coachman? I do say this fire feels lovely.'

'I would be delighted to join you. May I bring my invisible familiar Pillanitchskally?'

I nodded in agreement. Then came all cape and hair oblique in such a rush of inane laughter that I knew not what to think, but only for a gripping moment until I saw she had no blade nor pistol wielded. I had grown accustomed to the unusual with Charlotte, but secretly wished I could have taken this holiday alone, away from her— though I dare say the glen would have no longer been there upon my return. Burnt to a crisp it would have been; with all persons and animals dead for many miles round. This musing caused me to realize that I *did*, after all, see myself as a hero for the child; as her savior and guardian. This awareness came as a great surprise to me, and an epiphany heartening me in our hazardous plight.

'Round we go, round we go,' sang Charlotte as she circled her magic wand clockwise. 'Round we go, round we go, where we stop, where we slow, people wonder, and some know, yet round we go, round we go while Pillanitchskally jumps fast then slow.'

'That is a wonderful chant, Pinprick.'

'Bone-Snap wrote it.'

'Oh. I see. Well please relate to Bone-Snap that I find him a fine poet.'

'You can talk to him yourself, Mister Coachman.'

'Oh. Well. What a surprise.'

'Greetings John Coppe.'

I faltered, spilling hot tea on my thigh.

'Mr. Coppe? Be ye nervous?'

'Oh, no, Bone-Snap. Only a bit weary is all. It was a long ride through the night last.'

'Aye, it was. Nearly turned back did I, and thrice, for the cold wind in me eyes.'

How was I to talk to this strange being, or this part of Charlotte, or whatever it was? I pressed on.

'Found the wind crisp, did you Bone-Snap?'

'Oh, aye, sir. Crisp as a monkey's soul, truth be said. But I rode on, me faithful fellow travelers at me side.'

Crisp as a monkey's soul? I failed to see the connection between the two disparate ideas of 'chilly' and 'tropical,' but I chose not to belabor the point. In truth, I did not wish to be speaking with Bone-Snap, and sought passage out of the conversation.

'Your verse is quite good. Is Pinprick about, do you know?'

'Why thank thee kindly, sir, for the compliment on me poesy. And aye, she'd be just here. Pinprick, thy master wishes to talk with thee.'

I waited, a biscuit in my fingers to give Charlotte, but her features did not immediately change from the hardened Cromwellian soldier or fisherman or whatever Bone-Snap was supposed to be. Then, I watched awestruck as her visage changed like a rose blossom inverted in its natural course and come gradually back from the dead.

She began to weep.

'My love!' I cried. 'Come, sit with me.'

And she did so, but I was to soon find another creature sitting with me.

'Do you love me?'

It was Hallow— *Charlotte as a babe*. I gave her the biscuit I held, and she put it to her mouth, but did not chew with her teeth, rather with her lips as her spittle intermingled with her tears and dribbled in a thin stream down the side of her hand. I wiped away as much as I could, but the more I cared for her, the more she wept. Her frilly white sleeve was soon soaking.

'Pinprick,' I implored. 'Hallow?'

'Shut up, idgit!'

I jolted. Charlotte hopped away and drew her dirk. She then lowered her face at me and made slits of her eyes, her nostrils flaring in anger. I asked if I was now talking with Bloody-Tongue.

'Yes! We are haunted in here! What do you know of the ghost inside our house, Johnny boy! *Tell me!* I know you know something! *You must know something!*'

My thought now was that Charlotte, though indeed sharing her present life with the life of her early childhood in the form of Hallow, was not entirely splintered of mind, but was indeed possessed with some other entity altogether; a dead murderer, perhaps— or more than one. I knew little of her own life in Dublin, and wished to know much more, that I might better understand her. Yet, I burned to know of Bloody-Tongue and the other Green Shadows. And, were there more voices which had not yet come forth? I could not be at all sure, but wished to know this as well. If I was to have any hand in saving this wee girl, I had to know what possessed her. *I had to know them!*

'Bloody-Tongue,' said I. 'What are you frightened of?'

'The ghost, damn you! We are all afraid of it! Why do you reckon Hallow weeps? Because she wants her daddy? What a fool you are, Johnny boy!'

'Belay thy talk, Bloody-Tongue!'

Bone-Snap had returned.

'Aye, Bloody-Tongue. Shut it. *Now!*' I recognized the presence of Orange by the look on Charlotte's face— one of absolute maniacal turpitude much different than

Bone-Snap's hardened look or Bloody-Tongue's cynical twist of mouth and flashing eyes. Gloom, as I remembered, had seemed frightened, much like Hallow. I did not expect to hear from Gloom again.

Life had never been enjoyable with Charlotte, but now that I had succeeded in awakening the treasury of terror which was her mind, the idea of 'Hell' had taken on a new flavor for me. Living with 'Pinprick of Orange' was difficult enough. The addition of others, along with the lovable Charlotte when she was not being used by one or more of the stultifying gang, was making my life nearly intolerable. Something had to be done, yet I knew not what that thing might be. My voice had become a ghost inside her, which, as I had hoped, comforted her while frightening the others who had their claws imbedded in her so deeply. This was a fine beginning indeed. Yet, what would my next step consist of? Something had to be done, or our holiday at the shore— and my much-required time of rest— would fall to ruin. I chose the simplest answer to the dilemma.

'May I speak with Pinprick?'

'No!' replied Orange.

'Why may I not?'

No answer came forth.

'I ask again. Why may I not see Pinprick? I have built a fire for her, and I have biscuits and tea.'

Pinprick slashed her shortsword this way and that in a most menacing fashion, and began walking toward me.

'You are making me angry, Mister Coachman.' She calculated her steps through the sand like some kind of cold-blooded thing.

'Pinprick, I beg of you. Please be gentle. We are on holiday. Isn't it lovely to be away from the darkness of our glen and into full sunshine after so, so long? Remember that we have many days there when we never truly see the sun.'

'We see glimmers. Beautiful glimmers—'

I was making headway.

'Aye, the glimmers are beautiful,' I replied. 'Do you not love it when the light dapples the brook in the morning, or colors the leaves to varied shades of green?'

'Oh, so much, Mister Coachman!' Charlotte sheathed her sword and sat next to me.

'Pinprick?'

'Yes, Mister Coachman?'

'May I beg a favor from you?'

'Yes.'

(Ah, the trust of a child!)

'Pinprick, I do wonder if, while we are here at Bay Bretesche, you might ask your friends to rest awhile. Perhaps you could tell them that you would like to rest as well and enjoy the beach before you go back to work in the glen a few days hence. Do you believe you can do this for me— for us?'

'I believe so, Mister Coachman. So long as they don't hear your voice, but I can close the door so they won't be bothered by it. But, what about the others?'

I felt my eyes close in horror and disbelief. *The others?*

'What others, Pinprick?'

'There are yet others. They live in the attic.'

'I see. And where do the Green Shadows live?'

'In the cellar, of course.'

'These— *others*. What do they call themselves? Or, what do *you* call them?'

'Mister Coachman.'

'Yes, my love.'

'Your voice, after I open the door again, is going to scare the Green Shadows away. All except one.'

This strange knowledge of hers thrilled me. 'Might I guess which one?'

'Yes! I like guessing games!'

I decided to pretend that I did not know which would stay. Of course it would be Orange.

'Bloody-Tongue will remain,' I said.

'Ha! No.'

'Gloom?'

'Wrong again—'

'*Hmmm*, let me see,' I said as I tapped my chin with my finger and rolled my eyes. Pinprick was elated. Her eyes laughed as she giggled. Oh, how I loved her. How I loved that child.

'Bone-Snap?'

'You are getting warmer, Mister Coachman—'

'I have it now! Hallow. Hallow will stay.'

'Right! You guessed it right! It *is* Hallow!'

Could I be hearing wrong? My ears popped. I felt a great weight leave me. Yet, no. Surely she was jesting. Aye, that was it. My depression returned with immediacy. Yet, notwithstanding, I felt the need to query further.

'Did you say Hallow would be staying?'

'True that.'

'Are you teasing me, *mo croi?*'

'No. Why would you ask me that?'

'Oh, no reason,' I replied as I pulled Charlotte close and handed her a couple of biscuits. If she was telling the truth, Orange, who, as I understood it, had been the murderer within Pinprick, would be frightened away by my voice along with his three sordid cronies. Only Hallow would be left. Yet, what if I had miscalculated, and one, or more, of the voices in the attic had been Charlotte's 'evil twin' or somesuch. My dilemma was like searching for a haystack beneath a needle.

'Charlotte?'

'Yes, Mister Coachman?'

'What you say is true as true, then? Orange and his friends will be frightened of my voice when you open the door again, and only Hallow will stay?'

'Yes. But, Hallow will stay only if she wants to. She may not like to stay with Captain Malvapor living in the attic.'

'Captain Malvapor? Pray tell, who is he?'

'You know Captain Malvapor!'

'I do?'

'Yes, silly man! Captain Malvapor is the man in black who taught me how to shoot. Moreover, he becomes quite angry with you often. He likes skulls and severed heads and piratey things. And killing people. And other nasty things.'

Now the truth was told. I shivered with no control, though where we sat should have been warm to me. *Ach!* It was not only Orange who animated Pinprick toward devilish deeds. It was also this corrupt pirate Captain Malvapor, damn him! Why hadn't Charlotte allowed my voice— the ghost— into the attic? Or, had she?

'Pinprick? Does Captain Malvapor know of the ghost?'

'Yes. And he is terrified as well. All of my friends know of the spectre. None of them know it is you,

Mister Coachman. I have made sure of it, for I quite like the trick we are playing on them.'

'Does Captain Malvapor have mates?'

'Aye, he does. I don't know how many. A whole boatload, to be sure— but they are not as cruel as he. Some are mere lads my own age, some but a wee bit older. There are a number of girls as well. The Captain wears a thick beard, so he is much older than even you, I should think.'

'Will Captain Malvapor leave us be as well while we are holidaying here at Bay Bretesche? Could you ask him for this favor? He and his mates?'

'I will ask him. Yet, if he says no, then that means no. I would very much like for him to sleep a bit. He never sleeps, and that is why I think he is so ornery. My Uncle Gallian never sleeps, and I think that is why he hurts me so often.'

My God. The more I discovered about her life, the more I did not wish to know after all. Of a sudden, I had an idea. Chances were that it would not give the result I hoped for, but what did I have to lose? Absolutely nothing at all. My life was now Charlotte's; and I had already lost much of my sanity— a loss which allowed me to relate to her perhaps better than had I remained sane.

'Pinprick. Tomorrow is the day we celebrate the very

old season of Death—'

'*Hallow's Eve!* It's Hallows Eve? Oh, I adore this time of year!'

'Aye, then. And I know you enjoying pulling pranks. Would you like my voice, the ghost I am meaning, to really and truly frighten Captain Malvapor? Only as a jest, mind you. Another prank to couple with the one we are already playing.'

'Yes! *Yes!* Oh, how delightful! How shall we do it?'

'You will need to tell *me.*'

'*Hmm.* Alright, then, Mister Coachman. We had best be quick about it. He believes there is a plot against him, but he isn't quite sure what that might be as of yet. I do believe I know just the thing. He absolutely *hates* the society of children!'

As much as the action crushed my nerves, I needed to walk gently, for I knew, from experience, that Pinprick only became angry when I defied her, and my assumption, accordingly, was that my defiance brought Captain Malvapor roaring from his attic, pistols blasting, knives slicing. How could I have been so foolish to have believed, even for an instant, that Charlotte was being her sweet self as she killed with such precision; with such monstrous cruelty? One item was I sure of. She did not suffer. Living with these evil spirits, and with her wee splintered Hallow, was nothing other than a grand

game with her. Malvapor and the others saw to it that
they so fully embodied her that she was never frightened
of their violence, but thought it her own. *I* was the one
suffering. *I* was the one dying. It was evident to me that
if something did not happen, and rapidly, with this
abominable Captain Malvapor, and to a lesser degree
with the Green Shadows, I *would* die— and Charlotte
would not know what to do without me. As sorrowful a
situation as we found ourselves in, we were a team. I
could no more halt a racing coach-and-four alone and
relieve it of its treasures than could she maintain a
cottage and four horses alone— or, yet again, cross the
highway crying 'Stand and deliver!' and be taken with
any earnestness whatever. Yet, her chances as a nine-
year-old child were far worse than my own. Or, were
they? Perhaps Jacob Copper would take either of us into
his fold at the loss of the other. Aye, he would. I saw the
gentlemanly demeanor in his countenance the day he and
his men came for their half of our prize. Alas, alack—
my chances of leaving her with Copper and continuing
my life as a free man perished that fateful day. *God
damn this Captain Malvapor!* I would route him utterly,
and free us both of his petty tyranny, if it were the last
thing I ever accomplished. And then I might pray for his
soul. No, I *would* pray for him. I am not above
damnation myself. *Forgiveness.* I must remember

forgiveness.

†

'Pinprick? Are we ready then?'

'I do believe, Mister Coachman. You already met Hallow already. The names of the other children are Tumbling George, Violet, Polly, and Sinead.'

'Right, then. Hallow? Are you there? Tumbling George? Violet, where are you? Polly? Sinead, where are you hiding? Come out, come out wherever you are!'

Why of course! These were children I had heard playing in the glen! The penny finally dropped. Had they indeed been Charlotte (and Hallow), and this Tumbling George, Polly, Violet, and Sinead? Yes, yes they had! I felt euphoric. The Scripture 'and a little child shall lead them' sprang to mind, and mine eyes dimmed and oversprang with joyful tears.

'Why are you weeping?'

'Because I am happy, Pinprick.'

'My name isn't Pinprick. It is Violet. What might be *your* name, kind sir?'

I had not been certain that Charlotte's playmates were going to address me, yet at this point I found little in life to be disturbing.

'My name is John, my dear,' I replied. 'A happy Hallow's Eve to you.'

'I am pleased to meet you, Mr. John,' Violet said as

she curtsied. 'And a happy Hallow's Eve to you. Would you like to meet my sister Sinead, and our friends George and Polly?'

'Very much so. But first, please tell me. Might Charlotte and Hallow be somewhere near?'

'They are hiding, but I will call them if you like,' she said as she cupped her hands round her mouth. '*Hallow! Charlotte!* A nice gentleman is here asking for you!'

'Mister Coachman!' Pinprick cried, and I could see in her eyes that this was indeed my Charlotte.

'Pinprick, stay near as we play our trick, will you?'

'I will. But, you needn't call me that horrid name.'

I rocked back on my heels, but nodded, smiling as I said 'Right, then. Now, ah, *Charlotte*— gather your companions and go to the attic. Remember to make such a noise that the old scoundrel Malvapor knows not *what* to do! Does everyone have their masks in place? Is everyone ready for the attic?'

'Yes! Oh, this is so much fun, Mister Coachman! I so loathe Captain Malvapor! *Bye-bye!*'

Charlotte ran away, laughing the while, her witch-hair waving like an arrangement of wild grasses. Down the dunes to the shoreline she raced, and then along the lapping water's edge, where I watched her squat to study a seashell or somesuch other seaside thing. I saw that I would not be included in the jest, but found solace in my

hope that something would occur in favor of releasing
my girl from the satanic clutches of this repulsive man,
if indeed I could call him a man at all. And I had thought
the Woodmaster to be vile!

✝

I busied myself with making dinner as best I could
beneath our circumstances. Along with our biscuits and
tea, I managed to bring with us two dozen unbroken
eggs courtesy of the chickens who roam *Gleann na
Gruagh* at their leisure. Brought I as well fresh bread
and an array of dried meats, and a casting net so that we
might try our hands at angling, should the occasion
present itself. Benefitting from Charlotte's absence as
she played with 'the other children,' I went to the
shoreline myself and set about collecting cockles and
mussels, which I found to be innumerable, for steaming.
As I worked, though I tried, I could not keep from
imagining what was happening in 'the attic.' What news
would I be presented with upon Charlotte's return? My
thoughts even descended so far down as to think that she
may not return to me at all. Entangled in my attempts to
free her, I found that, after all, I was not, on this holiday,
a recipient of recreation as I had so hoped, but only the
uneasy John Coppe placed in a novel environ, and
perhaps even more dangerous situation. The glen
afforded us a dwelling to secrete ourselves while

providing for us a decided double-edged sword: a fear of the people— despite their societal positions— for what we had become, and a bounty of regular provisions. An open coastline, on the other hand, presented a variety of original, and not altogether comforting, possibilities. As one ensample, pirates and other equally nefarious ne'er-do-wells routinely combed this stretch for reasons known only to the soul hardened on the rolling deep. Alas! In seeking to do good for the both of us, had I inadvertently brought us into harm's way?

'Mister Coachman!'

'Charlotte?'

'No. Hello. It is Violet. Remember me?'

'Why of course, Violet. Where are the other children?'

'Just here with me.'

'What's up, sar,' said a boy's voice.

'And who would this be? Tumbling George, is it?'

'Aye, sar,' replied Charlotte as she puffed her chest out like a rough Dublin street urchin. 'At yer service, sar. What's oop?'

'Thank you, George. What news? Anything strange?'

'Aye, sar. I'll let Charlotte tell ye, sar. *Gorgeous* be what it be, sar.'

'Mister Coachman! We're back!'

I gazed into my girl's eyes. Yes, it was Charlotte.

'Tell me, then. What has occurred, *mo croi?*'[1]

'Oh, it was the most fabulous thing you ever saw! We sneaked up the stairs to the attic, our masks on so none of the other mates would notice us— they're used to seeing monsters everywhere— and then, with one grand yell, we rushed in and, and—'

'And? *And?*' I stood frozen. *Tell me!* I screamed within.

'Captain Malvapor was so frightened, he jumped through the pretty colored glass window and fell to his death below.'

I felt lightheaded. Vertigo threatened to overtake me. What had Charlotte now related to me? One of the very sources of her evil was— dead? Gone?

'Here, sit down, Mister Coachman,' said a new, more mature, and very friendly voice. 'I am Violet's elder sister Sinead. I am nine years old, like Charlotte.'

I did as I was told, and soon had a steaming cup of tea in my hand and a plate of biscuits next to me.

'There is one of you I have not yet met,' I finally said from my delirium. 'Polly, is it?'

Charlotte giggled, and then pinched my arm quite hard.

'Charlotte! That smarts!'

'It wasn't me, Mister Coachman. That was Polly!

---

[1] my heart

Tee-hee!'

'Oh, well— in *that* case—'

'She likes you, Mister Coachman,' said Charlotte. 'She might tell you herself, but she is quite bashful. Wait—'

I waited.

'Mister Coachman? The children all wish you a wondrous Hallow's Eve, and are sorry to say it, but they would like to leave for a bit. They have a bit of haunting to do elsewhere.'

'And, what about Hallow? Is she here with us?'

'Yes. Hallow has decided to stay. She is fast asleep just now.'

'And, the other Green Shadows? Where are they?'

'Off a'haunting.'

'When— will they return? Do you know?' I asked, feeling cold, feeling terrified yet of Orange and Bloody-Tongue and, yes, even of Bone-Snap. The greatest tyrant was gone, or so I had been told. But these smaller despots, *ach!* Charlotte for some reason saw them as her companions.

'I never know when they will be here, Mister Coachman. They come and go as they please.'

'Charlotte, are you aware that some of your mates are quite rude to me?'

'Aye, and I am sorry of that, Mister Coachman. I'm

only afraid of them sometimes.'

'If you are afraid of them, my love, why allow them to live with you?'

'Because from time to time they are amusing to be with, and Orange also knows how to shoot quite well. And *he* makes me laugh a lot.'

My blood ran cold. It wasn't over. Orange was a murderer. And I reckoned that Bloody-Tongue, and perhaps even Bone-Snap, had their hands soiled on more than the rare occasion. I was peering into a glass darkly. No, it wasn't over. The war had not yet ended. I wanted to say something to the effect that Charlotte had other playmates she also enjoyed playing with; friends of whom I fully approved. But I bit my tongue, for the wee girl had grown drowsy. I pulled her into my lap, and soon enough she was sleeping soundly.

†

'Charlotte. Wake up, sweet one.'

'*Hmmm?* Ach! You called me Charlotte! You are making me angry, Mister Coachman!' She reached for my pistol. I knocked it from her fingers. She winced and slapped at me, her fingernails scratching my jaw. Then she fell silent.

I felt my head shaking from side to side, but it was as if I were not me in truth, but someone or some *thing* else having invaded me, or turned me inside out, or taken me up and about and then dropped me from some great height so that I lost myself in the fall, and died, but did not die. Is this understood? Is my meaning clear? I was indeed dying, or perhaps I was dead already, and living in Hell. Perhaps I had been killed on the road to the Proorice mansion, and this was my punishment for having lived a life of youthful selfishness. Youthful selfishness? No, I had been a good lad, honorable to my parents, a gentleman in society. I was being punished for something different; for something I had done that I knew not; some grand 'sin of omission' which had sent me instantly to Hell. There was no love in the world. There could *be* no love in the world. *Love?* Where was there love? There was no love. No. There was no love. There was no God, no Sacrifice— nothing at all except undying pain.

'I love you, Mister Coachman. I am exceedingly sorry about Orange. He came back. I told him to go lie down for a bit. He obeys me sometimes, but usually only when he has drank too much. *I got drunk last night, dear mo-ther! I'm drunk again to-day!'*

I stared straight ahead. I felt my saliva slithering from my lower lip, but I wanted to do nothing about it. I felt overheated. I felt chilled. I was thirsty. The idea of drinking water made me want to hang myself. I longed for sleep. The notion of closing my eyes made me wish to scratch them out. I began to laugh, yet nothing was humorous. I began to weep, yet I was not sad. I laughed and wept together, and neither action was connected to its proper emotion. I looked down at my hands. My fingernails were long like a mole's claws. My boots were gone, and in place of my feet I had cloven hooves. I smelled burning brimstone. I was Satan now, I reckoned. Satan tortured in Hell for his crimes against mankind, against God, against himself and all the angels.

'Mister Coachman!'

Her voice sounded distant. 'Charlotte? Is that you? Look at my feet! Are they not comical? And my hands. See? Claws instead of fingers now.'

'Mister Coachman! I know what has happened! Gloom has gotten inside your head! *Gloom!* Leave Mister Coachman be! Leave him be! *Out!*'

It was then I heard a great popping noise, as if a loose sail had snapped in a brisk wind. I jolted to a standing position from where I sat humped over, and of a sudden did not know where I was. My eyesight dimmed, and I remember stumbling about like a blind man without his cane, my hands flailing in front of me, my legs crossing one another in a perilous ballet.

'Gloom! *I said out!*'

I fell topsy-turvy over a dune, scooping up wet sand into my mouth as I fell. Be that so, I lay there, helpless, until Charlotte came to me and, with great exertion, helped me back to my feet.

'Spit it out! Spit all of that sand out! Here's some water for you. You are not well, Mister Coachman. You should lie down. In our tent. Under loads of blankets.'

'Sank you, Psinspick, but I freel—'

Those were the last words I said, I do believe, before the sky above was suddenly at my left, and then at my right, and then below me.

The dream which I remembered when I awoke displayed a ghastly pastiche of my life back in Dublin where, in one scene, I was not a young house servant freshly educated and ready to work my way toward being head steward of some estate. No. Rather, I was a piece of crumpled parchment paper forgotten next to a lord's desk, eventually picked up by a servant of the house and thrown into a roaring fireplace. As I crackled and burned, becoming ash and smoke, I thought, *So, this is what my life has come to? To live, to feel alive, to believe I understand life and have purpose for living, only to be crushed in some egoist's fingers and tossed aside for the flames.*

Another part of my dream had me living as a poor child on the streets of Dublin begging for monies and food, begging for clothes and shelter from the bitter cold. I had known, and played with, such children in reality. My father, an artisan of Stoneybatter, where I was born and raised, taught me to love everyone regardless of social position, teaching me that each station has its difficulties, and that each station also has its petty tyrants. No one is omitted from the human game of either learning to become one of them, or escaping the cycle through the Sacrifice of Jesus into perfect freedom and peace of mind.

An other part of my dream had me living as a horse. I remember that I was a gelding solely dependent upon my master for everything, and in exchange for his kindnesses to me I was required to take him everywhere he wanted to go. I remember the weight of him on my back, and his gentle words to me sometimes; and I wished that he were a much lighter man.

Finally I died, and went to a place of gnawing worms and unconsuming fire. The pain was agonizing, yet I could not die, hard as I tried to 'give up the ghost.' Then it dawned upon me— the most brutal horror I had yet ever been recipient of: I had already died, my spirit had already left my earthy body, and my new condition would be a permanent one throughout a timeless eternity.

✝

I was awakened by the strong yet delightful scent of baking fish. I lay for a spell, trying, with much prayer, to pull myself back in concert, and when I finally was able to piece together that I lay in our tent beneath several blankets, and that all of my clothing had been removed, I rose and took in the fresh, chilly November beach air.

'Pinprick, where are my trousers?'

'Drying here by the fire. I washed them. They should be dry by now. And, I am Charlotte again.'

When I was dressed, I joined Charlotte and was handed a platter of roasted *twaite shad*, a delicious fish found in abundance in the area.

'Charlotte, how will I know when you are Charlotte and when you are Pinprick?'

'I should be sent to Bedlam, Mister Coachman. You *won't* know.'

'Then, I must call you 'Pinprick' at all times hereafter. Is this acceptable to you, Pinprick?'

'Aye, it is I do reckon. Do you like the fish I cooked for you?'

'Very much indeed. I have always loved twaite, when I could get some. What will we do today?'

'I have begun a sand castle which needs finished. Would you like to help me, Mister Coachman?'

'I can think of no better fun in the entire world.'

Her beaming smile and dancing eyes brought tears to my own.

†

The walls of the fort she built with her hands. For turrets— and there were four— she used one of our drinking cups as a mould. Twigs punched through leaves served as castle banners. A thin piece of driftwood had been placed as the drawbridge. The moat was fed by the ocean tide. Because the structure was built of seashells, the water did not destroy the castle with its approaches. I dare say the Anglo-Norman installation which gave Bay Bretesche its name would not have seemed as fine a creation in my eyes, and I told Charlotte so. This made her blush and giggle, but she said not a word in reply, which caused me to wonder if perhaps Hallow was doing most of the work. I did not query concerning this, however, but continued with my project of extending the castle wall toward the mainland, which Charlotte did not seem to mind in the least. My goal was to create a corral of a kind, and then to populate it with twig horses and sheep. But, we were retarded in our venture by a mighty act of God. A storm swept upon us with such purple fury that, though enjoying ourselves thoroughly, we exerted ourselves to near exhaustion by merely gathering up Charlotte's fish and our varied belongings and getting it all into the tent before the deluge— which did come with a Biblical vengeance.

†

Next day brought the lovely warmth of sunshine to us

again, and a surprise visit from an acquaintance.

'Mister Coachman,' said Charlotte as her features hardened. 'How long must we stay in this open land? I do not like it here whatsoever. We can be seen for miles in either direction, and also from the water, should someone be interested. And they usually are.'

Without thinking, I replied, 'You, Bone-Snap, need not stay for any length of time. Go at your leisure, my good man.' I nearly added the words *You will not be missed*, but caught myself in time, realizing that this entity carried such a low opinion of himself that any idea he may not be wanted could lodge him even deeper into Charlotte's soul.

Her features softened. 'Bone-Snap said he was leaving, Mister Coachman. He said to tell you he didn't know when he would be back, and is sorry if your work in the glen suffers in his absence.'

'Well, I am grateful for his assistance,' I replied, trying hardily not to laugh aloud, 'and I am sure his helping hand shall sorely be missed. Relate this to him should you see him again, will you Pinprick? By the by, any word from Bloody-Tongue? Or my good friend Gloom? And, what of Orange this fine day? How does *he* spend his time?'

'Oh! I quite forgot to tell you! When the children and I found our way into the attic, we discovered Bloody-

Tongue in conference with Captain Malvapor over somesuch pirate raid or other— some famous thing they had done together in years passed, on the island they called Mad-as-a-hatter.'

Madagascar? My mind suddenly reeled. Was this— could this actually have been the infamous pirate Captain *Hieronymous* Malvapor? And Bloody-Tongue. Who in God's Name was this Bloody-Tongue? *The penny dropped!* Piracy has always been of particular interest to me. I have read many accounts, and from my studies did I suddenly remember that the chosen quartermaster of Malvapor, a particularly cruel and altogether amoral miscreant by the name of Charles Ibbard, had come to be known, *aye!* as *Bloody-Tongue* for a fight he had with an unnamed helmsman who, during a savage loggerheads, bit off a piece of his tongue in the attempt to silence the rabid animal. Both Malvapor and Ibbard were eventually captured and hanged at Execution Dock, at Wapping, where, among other notorious villains, the privateer-turned-pirate Capt. William Kidd was hanged.

I told none of what I knew to Charlotte.

'Anyway,' she continued, 'when we frightened Captain Malvapor so badly that he jumped through the window and died, Bloody-Tongue, trying to save his mate from suicide, sliced his own arm on the broken glass and, with no one there to help him, he died soon thereafter, his blood spurting everywhere, even all over us children!'

The notion of a rotting ghost lying in Charlotte's attic repulsed me to no end. I sat shuddering with horror and wondering if his body might now bring her gangrene of the mind.

'Did you leave Bloody-Tongue's corpse where it fell?'

'Oh, no, Mister Coachman! We picked it up and tossed it from the window after Captain Malvapor. We laughed when we heard their skulls crack together. It was like something of a wee *pop!* Hee-hee.'

I was so relieved at this happy report that I got up from where I sat and raced down the shoreline, fairly screaming at the top of my lungs 'Now I have merely Gloom and Orange to contend with! Only these two scoundrels left! One to send me to Bedlam, and the other to, well, *yes!* to send me to Bedlam! Oh, what a happy, delirious, saddened man I am! *Ha-ha-ha-ha-ha!*'

†

'Just over the way there is a house, Mister Coachman. We will burgle it.'

'Pinprick, my doll, we are not housebreaks.'

'*Arrg!* You *shall* break in with me, Mister Coachman. They have silverplate there! I just *know* it!

107

And fine food! And dolls and toys! Do you wish to make me angry? I will slice you!'

'Orange!' cried I. 'I have enjoyed quite enough of your bullying, sirrah! If you will spread your tyranny round, take it elsewhere, for I will no longer countenance your insisting this and demanding that!'

Charlotte looked at me dumbfounded, her mouth agape, her eyes wide with surprise. For this expression, I knew that I gazed into the eyes of Orange, who had never once expected me to stand up to his back-ally antics. Of a sudden unfreezing, he drew his dirk and advanced toward me. Therefore, I drew my own weapon and brandished it. Being the more superior fighter of the two of us, meaning myself and *Charlotte*, I quickly disarmed Orange with a move I had been forced to practice in Stoneybatter from childhood. Charlotte wore a brace of pistols tucked into her belt, but these were not drawn on me. Why? *Of course!* Orange had *never* drawn guns on me, the coward! It had always been Captain Malvapor, or perhaps Bloody-Tongue— or even Bone-Snap. My God! This arrangement, or disarrangement as it more likely were, would have been enough to drive the simplest man to full lunacy.

What, I wondered, was Orange's weight with Charlotte? I reckoned that he was mean of mouth, as were they all save Hallow and the woodland children, but he acted as the cruel one to animals. Was he also inhospitable to people? I was conjecturing, hoping to be correct in my assumption. Yet, could not an evil spirit change while living in Hell; become even more wicked along his journey through the Land of Corruption? I was not willing to believe for an instant that Orange was fully set in his ways and could not take on for himself the perversities of Malvapor and that ignominious Bloody-Tongue. I reminded myself, to a moment of deep consolation, that I had but Orange and Gloom to vie with, hoping that my prayers against the return of Bone-Snap would be answered; believing the Scripture promising that 'the effectual fervent prayer of a righteous man avails much.' I, a righteous man? Purely relative, of course, but in our particular condition, aye, I was indeed a righteous man. A very righteous man indeed.

I found Charlotte behind a sand dune, weeping as if she had lost her only friend.

'I am frightened.' She reached for my hand.

'Be not afraid. We shall make it through this, as we have made it through every other challenging circumstance thus far.'

'I love you, Mister Coachman.'

'And I love you, Pinprick.'

✝

The following morning, just after daybreak, Charlotte and I left Bay Bretesche. Our journey back to the glen proved itself as eventful as our escape had been uneventful, as I shall now relate in as much detail as I can.

7

Bring the Asofetida

'Ho there! State thy business, sir!'

It was a gentleman farmer walking his land no doubt, by the look of him in his sharp maroon-colored hat and matching suit of clothes.

I replied to the man. 'My name is John Abernathy, kind sir. And this is my daughter Matilda traveling with me this fine day. We have this morning come up from holiday on Bay Bretesche, and seek a shorter path back to the highway and then to our home in Rathmines.'

'I see. Well, surely I mind not thee on the land, Master Abernathy. 'Tis the way of this great island, as I reckon thou knowest well, hearing thy North Dublin brogue. It be thy *geldings* I mind, sir, traipsing the land. Only sheep stroll this meadow. Me own horses hast their own pasture, as do me bovine stock theirs. I'll ask thee to cut across just there, sir,' he said as he pointed toward a nearby copse of young ash. 'Once through the trees, kick the stone wall down, replace it upon thine egress, and kindly be on thy way.'

I doffed my own hat (a wide-brimmed monstrosity not dissimilar to that of the gentleman farmer), nodded, and turned my mount. Charlotte followed my lead, saying not a word to the man as we left him to his estate.

It is best that when in Rome, relate as the Roman. It was
for this reason that we had taken great care not to outfit
ourselves as highwaymen whilst on the road.

In short time we rode the highway back home to the
glen, but Lady Fortune would not be with us as had she
the night we left for our beach recreation, if I may call
those days of disquiet such.

'Mister Coachman, my mount has lost a shoe.'

This meant that we had to stop and examine his hoof,
which we did. I found no severe damage, but the result
of this misadventure was that we could not gallop for
any reason whatever, even to save our lives. Our pace
was now forced to be measured with great care until we
arrived home. What I would do about the shoe at that
juncture, I knew not, and could not at that time afford
much expenditure of thought on the matter. The nearest
blacksmith resided in the coastal village of *Na Clocha
Liatha* not far away, but it might as well have been a
lifetime away for a felon like myself ripe for the
'hempen dance' as it were! Perhaps there were extra
shoes in the old stable, and some nails, and a hammer.
The prospect of shoeing a horse unnerved me.

'Ride carefully,' I told Charlotte. 'Watch for jagged
stones, and avoid them. If he begins to limp, let me
know without delay. Other than this, I know not what to
tell you on the matter. We shall be home shortly, barring

other incident.'

We plodded on in silence until I was hungry and asked Charlotte if she might like to stop and eat something. She was not hungry, she said, and did not wish us to stop. I gave pause, and surmised that I was speaking again with either Gloom or Orange, for the *real* Charlotte would have thought of my own need for sustenance, and also of our horses in need of rest and food, and halted without more ado. And, since, to my mind, it was Gloom who seemed to have taken a liking to my *own* personality, the remaining culprit was Orange. Would I ever be rid of these vermin? *Ach!*

On we rode, taking side paths as often as possible, though these were likely sheep trails possibly populated by accompanying sheep and their shepherds. We found luck, however, and until we sighted the first trees of the glen up ahead, near dusk, we encountered no more local resistance, whatever that may have consisted of. This turn of fortune could have been in large part to Charlotte's red riding hood and my own choice of cloaks— a splendid green beauty sporting a cream silk lining. Not the usual blacks, drabs, and dowdies of the working footpad.

'Mister Coachman,' said Charlotte, breaking a lengthy silence. 'We are lost.'

What was she saying? Could she not see our forest

treeline up ahead? Pulling myself from a reverie where I was again with my family in Dublin, as a younger man during the always-happy Christmas season, I looked about us. Charlotte was accurate. Ahead lay not *Gleann na Gruagh* as I had earlier seen it, but rather a great expanse of meadow, spreading for what seemed miles on all sides of us. I checked the saunter of my mount. No, we were not on bog-land, thank God. Where were we? How had we come to this place in such quick time? I did not at all recognize the lie of the land, though the flora was indeed Irish enough. Round us grew gorse with their infernal thorns, clumps of thatching reed here and there, tall grasses blowing in the wind, ferns waving their cheerful salutes, stands of nettle facing docks in the eternal war between them— all part of the usual Hibernian flora.

It was then that Charlotte and I were unexpectedly covered with tiny warriors who climbed, lassoed, and galloped on miniature warhorses (many of them with wings!) and yelled outlandish epithets to one another, to which the recipients of such strange nicknames would turn their mounts in one direction or another, depending on the present need. From every possible direction they swarmed like midges in a springtime calm! My first horrifying thought was that the Woodmaster had in some way returned from the dead, and these were more of his fetid miniscule creatures come to dispatch us.

Soon we were both tied to our own mounts with lengths of hempen cord, our horses themselves halted all round by the sheer number of the wee populace of this field.

I knew not what to say, and so I sat dumbfounded.

One of the men stepped forward, and as he did so, he was suddenly grown to normal human height. 'I am Ainm,' he greeted with a genuine smile as he shifted his lustrous brown cloak aside to show that he was frightfully armed. 'We are in search of a being who has caused our people great harm.' He eyed Charlotte up and down.

'Mister Coachman! Those wild men are looking at me weirdly! I am frightened!'

'Sir!' I cried. 'What is the meaning of this foolishness? Can you not see that we are weary travelers in search of no activity which would put our lives into the Devil's clutch?'

'I will ask you to be silent sir, you and your charge alike, until I have said my piece.'

With those words, before our eyes the tens of thousands of miniature heathen amalgamated into an hundred and more fully sized warriors. The wildest and daftest thought I believe I have ever had was that I could take fifty of them down with ease, leaving Charlotte the rest to lay low in her ferocity. As I thought this, all of them laughed aloud, as if hearing my every inner word.

'We do hear you, sir,' spoke Ainm. 'Your musings are not hidden from us, for we are Cumhacht, and being so, we act as one and know as one. Yet, as our lives are led by joyous ceremony and great revel, we will simply take him that we seek and allow you to be on your way. There is a method, though, that we shall follow in our ascertainment of the blackguard.'

Here I should slow in my narrative and seek to give in greater feature the appearances of these men; these feral *Cumhacht*. For in all of my knowledge gained through reading and listening to the old ones tell their tales of our ancients on this island, never had I heard of such beings, of such dress, of such demeanor. If I will tell of them, perhaps it will be better understood why we went without strife with them, and the reason that Charlotte appeared to become quickly at ease. Under similar circumstances we may have fought (though in vain against our ropes) and brought our health to an unsatisfying low, as is usual with captives held against their wills. Not so in this case. The leader proved congenial, and though his many warriors could, it seemed to me, destroy any human regiment with their mere gazes, they also showed themselves to be more than genteel to the both of us. I will tell now of these figures comprehensively, if not for pure entertainment and recapitulation alone.

Flanking the man called Ainm, on either side of him, stood six Cumhacht, numbering twelve in all, making him the thirteenth of their *avant garde*. All of them— the entire horde of them— smelled of burning turf and cinnamon-baked apples. Never a more delicious olfactory blend.

The six Cumhacht to Ainm's sinister side were dressed in rich blue *bracchae* and matching cloaks; the six to his right stood barefoot and clad in vermilion kilts alone. He himself, as I have described, wore a wonderful brown cloak, which was clasped with a golden brooch formed in the shape of a round battle shield.

The blue-cloaked men wore their hair cropped so that a myriad of spikes stood like thorns from their scalps, and in my mind's eye I saw ripened apples fall upon the heads of them and rest there, impaled. Their eyes were grey-green almonds, made fierce with the winds of change and surely with the caprice of mankind ever invading their world. The weapons of this sinister guard were the arrow and the *shillelagh*.

Their brothers, to the right of Ainm and arrayed in vermilion, too had almond eyes (as did all the others in this field), but these eyes were a shadowy blue, yet also ferocious and unrelenting in their power. The hair of this

six grew long, and in color was dark-gold, and naturally
waved with tighter curls where it fell across their
shoulders. They sported no apparent weapons, yet they
each wore two long crystals sheathed in leathern
pouches like dirks, and I knew because of this that they
were of magical battle technique, and feared them far
more than the crop-haired men of martial might.

As I studied closer, I saw, to both my astonishment
and consolation (for we Irish were once egalitarian to a
fault), that fully half of the warriors I firstly thought to
be male were women! I so wanted to speak out, to
applaud this ancient Gaelic picture so uncommon in the
world, but found myself dumb. Turning to Charlotte, I
saw that she sat fully enraptured by the spectacle about
us. Her countenance fairly glowed with enthusiasm as
we rested, bound captives, on our 'midnight moonless
mounts' as Charlotte called our horses.

'Bring the asofetida,' commanded Ainm, yet before
any soul could have possibly heard him and responded,
two of the women were tying to our horses bags of a
fetid substance so that these hung just below the muzzles
of the animals. I choked and gagged as the breath and
saliva of my horse moistened the foul contents. I would
soon find that it was a dusty brown powder as it
collected about the animals' nostrils. They did not snort
nor step foot. Charlotte held her hand over her face, yet

her watering eyes smiled. She giggled then, and Ainm turned his attention to her, his eyes gazing deeply. Our hempen bonds were cut from us by two more female warriors.

The women were outfitted like the men, and all wore their long hair (of various natural hues) brought up and tied close to their napes. Yet, the differences in them are here described.

The women from which the bringers of the asofetida came were arrayed in ochre which I found beautiful set against their peach-toned skin. Even their boots were of this lustrous color. Lapis eyes had they, and each moved with quick and even step, though she were tall in stature. Their weapons? Short staves sheathed in leather on their backs.

The women cutting our bonds were dark of coloring, like full-blood Gypsies, their eyes shining like stones of obsidian. As weapons they had tucked into their belts wands carved of whitethorn. These warriors, smaller of stature than all the rest of their people, moved more furtively; and the two of them releasing us were then three, and then one, and then four.

A third group of women wore both red and green, and were decorated with holly and ivy, and bore as weaponry oaken lances with silver heads glimmering in the sunlight. Their eyes were pale blue like water from a cataract, their hair golden as baked bread, their skin apple-flesh white, their bodies willowy and strong.

As we sat upon our mounts, seemingly suspended in time, as if in a dream, my attention then turned to the remaining warriors, all male, which at once seemed five score, and then but half that number, and then a plethora uncountable. But firstly, of the horses of our captors, a sight in and of itself worth relating.

The horse of Ainm, as with all of them, was armored in gold plate; its golden headdress and partial mask transforming it into a wolf.

The sinister guard of Ainm rode animals who, for their intricately smithed golden design, were carrion crows.

The right-hand guard rode horses that had been transformed into hares.

The ochre women were mounted upon many-pronged stags.

The dark women, those like Gypsies, rode sea-dogs.

The women of green and red sat upon equine badgers.

The remaining divisions had their horses transformed into adders, salmon, boar, big cats, goats and, of all creatures, tarpans. All of the horses appeared to be perfectly comfortable masquerading as other creatures. If I were a horse, I might not wish to be a hare or a goat, a salmon or a tarpan. But I am not a horse, and so I cannot rightfully say one way or the other.

One group of warriors presented themselves unreservedly naked and covered in woad, a blue paint made from *isatis tinctoria*, or the common glastum plant. Printed upon their woad, or perhaps permanently dyed into their skin beneath it, were simple figures of animals, and sometimes only of animal footprints such as those of the wolf, the boar, and the raven. These warriors wore their golden hair cut shaggily in various layers, and it hung long to their belts, and was adorned with peregrine feathers and beads made of wood and stones. An untamed quality emanated from their eyes golden-green like those of a certain cats. They were armed with the bow and arrow, and with fighting sticks.

Another set of armed men were fortified with throwing axes and nothing else, but each man wore three of them.

I spoke to Ainm, unable to keep myself from it. 'You seem such a peaceable people. I do not feel any animosity from you, and please believe me, sir, if there were fear with you causing feelings of anger, I would know it. Yet—'

'Ah. Our weapons,' he replied with a nod. 'Are these that which you make reference to? If so, understand that we are not men, and so being, you and your girl see what you are most accustomed to seeing. Each of these weapons are not weapons at all, but are qualities which compare to the *personalities*, shall we say, of your sword, your dirk, your arrow, and so on. Not physical at all in the sense of human physicality, but no less formidable. The same is for us. We do not necessarily wear long hair, or short hair, or ochre, red, or dun. We do not of necessity even *have* hair to wear in this style or that, or heads to wear that hair upon. We do not necessarily ride horses. We do not necessarily ride at all, yet travel we do, but perhaps not as do men. The mind is a beautiful, powerful thing. What it believes comes true, is made real, in every instance, be that belief hellish, or celestial. Selfish, or selfless.'

I wanted to understand his words of explanation (and much later did so, to a degree), yet I found myself more enthralled with what I saw before and about us than what these beings really were, if they were indeed what their leader said they were— entities other than mankind. At this time, I did not know, but I sensed that they were of the Middle Kingdom— yet I did know this: We were their captive audience. We could have developed wings and flown away from them with far more ease than we could have ridden away.

Yet another passel of armed men wore masks. Of these six I was most frightened, but of the same I saw that Charlotte was most fascinated. They wore red and black tartan bracchae[1] and matching cloaks clasped with silver brooches formed like small harps.

One disguise was of a man with a bloodied face, as if he had been beaten to death in a fit of rage.

A second was of an ancient woman, the tip of her nose touching her lower lip, her wiry grey hair reaching out in all directions like dead twigs on a dead tree branch.

A third combatant wore the face of Jack-in-the-Green, but from his mouth erupted not lively foliage but a woman's long bloody fingers, tender and unworked in life.

Yet another— a fourth— was a horsemen sporting the countenance of a screaming girl-child, her face twisted with terror.

Still another wore the mask of Death; a skull hooded in black.

'Ho! Ho!' cried a sixth, his head then toppling from his shoulders altogether— or, so it seemed. A magnificent deception indeed! I shuddered.

If these 'men of the masque' were not enough— if my mind were not spinning enough— ten ermine-clad soldiers rode into the midst of all and dismounted. They then faced one another, broadswords drawn, for combat,

---

[1] breeches

five squared against five. Charlotte looked worried, therefore I knew that neither Gloom nor Orange had made decision to reawaken in her. Were they frightened of this juggernaut of warriors? If they were not, I knew of no good reason why. In truth, I knew of no human army, no matter how massive or renowned, who would not blench in their presence.

No combatant spoke, but rather eyed his foe with a piercing gaze and moved toward him, unrelenting in his step. These, I might add, wore lengthy hair the color of cinnamon, and it flew freely in the breeze like fingers of fire. This would be a contest to the death. Death? Could these warriors die?

'*Doirt!*' cried Ainm.

'Pour out'? His word meant to pour something out. Blood was to pour surely, yet this man had already shown himself to know things not common, and so I savored his word, thinking it surely meant more than a declaration of the obvious. It would, sure, coming from a man whose name meant 'Name,' and whose people's name meant 'Power.'

A first hack from one was parried by the neck of his opponent, and then there were nine wearing the resulting spew of lifeblood. The contest came to an abrupt halt as these remaining formed a loose ellipse round their beheaded brother. Ainm took the head up from where it rolled, tied it to his baldric by its hair, and went to stand next to the body. I became that much more colder as the next stage unfolded.

'*He that we seek*

comes as one meek!' spake the dispatched head as it hung.

'*Yet one knows here*

that he brings fear.

More hundreds know that with false cross

he blasphemes He who embraced loss,

He who poured out,

He who raised all

with red and pall

up from the Fall.'

I know nothing, I whispered to myself. *Nothing at all. He who poured out?*

'Stand, great warrior,' commanded Ainm as he untied the man's head from his person. 'Walk amongst us again in the Kingdom.'

My dear God, thought I. *All of this may be damaging to Charlotte!* Then I remembered that she had partaken in crimes far more hideous than the beheading of a man, and I glanced to her. Indeed, she sat silent and looking on with keenness as if watching a play being performed—and perhaps she was at that.

The dead warrior stood, walked to Ainm, took his head, placed it upon his shoulders, and, save the blood soaking his clothing, all was again as if no blade had cut through muscle and bone.

'Further!' cried Ainm then, and, with Charlotte and I flanked by a fresh set of warriors wearing white gossamer gowns and helmets of silver engraved with the images of wolves, we all began to move in unison across the field. The excitement of the death and rebirth, or the 'pouring out,' must have mystified me, for once again the atrocious odor of the asofetida wafted up from below so that with great difficulty did I not become nauseous. My concentration now upon my rolling belly, I realized that I was not at all hungry, though surely I should have been by this time.

'I am not hungry either, Mister Coachman,' said Charlotte, and I knew then, without doubt, that we rode through the Middle Kingdom.

As we moved along, the pasture became dappled with the shadows of racing clouds, and of a sudden we were beneath a cobalt blue canopy which spanned the sky in all directions. The scent of rain lay heavy on the air, and sunset began, but into the East. A mirror world. *Of course*. Why would it be otherwise?

Presently there lay before us a glen far more open than our home of *Gleann na Gruagh*, seeming much

more like the nearby *Gleann dá Locha* in its expanse.
Here we halted, and Charlotte and I were handed from
our mounts. The ground beneath me felt solid and sure,
and I soon was at full ease among this strange folk. Yet
no sooner stood I at peace than there came a great
howling on the approaching night. Charlotte ran to me
and held to me.

'Wolves,' said I. 'Fear not, dear *cailín*. We are firmly
protected by our new friends here, I believe, should the
animals hunger for something other than their
accustomed fare.'

'Would it be likely that we are attacked this eve?'
asked Ainm of me. ' I say not. The land of the Cumhacht
knows no imbalance as does your own world where
wolves sup upon sheep and small children for dearth of
deer— deer kept for the pleasure of your selfish
monarchs and noblemen.'

'Mister Warrior?' asked Charlotte addressing Ainm.
'What are the foul-smelling bags hung round our horses
mouths for?'

'You shall see, child,' replied the leader and
spokesman in a most gentle tone. 'First, I welcome you
both to Hall Scáthanna.'

Then round us stood wooden walls high and
impenetrable, and we were within a broad hall lit with
white candles set in golden sconces. The place was

warmed with a huge stone hearth which could have fit twelve men standing in comfort. I could not help but recognize this structure from descriptions of the magnificent hostels built by our ancients on this isle such as that of the notorious witch-warrior Nemhthenga, or the famous House of the Dagda where friend and foe alike could eat his fill and rest in perfect peace.

The howling of the wolves came again— closer to us now. Charlotte reached for my hand. Then a great door was flung wide, and we peered out into the purple dusk to see at first shadows, and then ghosts, and then fuller formed shapes— wolves— bringing themselves into the hall. I counted. There were eleven in number when the portal shut behind them. I saw then that our horses had not been stabled, but stood with us all. The leader of the wolves spoke. 'Asofetida we smell. You have called us, friend Ainm. What is it that you seek?'

'We have found him, Ceannaire,' replied Ainm.

'Ah! What news is this? You have found the rebel? Well done, my lord!'

'Well done indeed,' said two or three of the other wolves in unison.

'Where is he?' asked Ceannaire as he looked to Charlotte with knowing eyes.

'We have not yet removed him. We await your guidance.'

The wolves circled as if in conference. We waited, and in their time Ceannaire came again to the forefront. 'You know,' he said matter-of-factly. 'All of you know, save the man and the girl, that there is but one way to extract him. That you have him in our midst stands nothing short of a wonder. I dare say that in time he shall escape again, and that his flagitious comrades, in his absence, shall hold his keep. Yet, *this* day you have him, for you do not tell untruths. And that you have him shows us all that belief, if held to fervently, avails much.'

'Aye,' replied all, and their unified agreement shook the very pillars which supported the rafters and ceiling.

I held not an inkling of what was transpiring, and I shook with fear for the lack of knowledge. My knees nearly gave way beneath me.

'Sir,' spoke Ainm as he turned to me. 'A word with you in privy.'

I stepped toward him to oblige, but with a wave of his hand he stopped me.

'Unnecessary, sir. I can speak directly to your mind. What I have to say will not seem at all pleasant, however.'

I was then flanked by two outsized warriors. They did not touch me, but stood close to me as one of the women took Charlotte by the hand and led her to a seat, where she was then attended by other women. They gave her what appeared to be Welsh rarebit to eat, and spoke to her in soft tones until she smiled.

'Sir and good guardian of the sweet girl-child,' continued Ainm. 'I address you as but spokesman of all here tonight, Cumhacht and wolf-lord alike. The girl you carry in your charge is the purloined abode of one sometimes called Gloom. We know she has in passed times housed others, and houses others yet. But it is Gloom that we seek, for he stands as constant adversary of all that is rightwise, and has brought untold sorrow to many. Do you know him, sir?'

'I do know him,' I replied from within my mind, as speaking this way came with an unexpected ease. 'He is a madman, a ghost of some breed who took me not three days ago and rung my mind as if it were a wet rag. I despise him.'

'Know you more of him?'

'Nothing. Should I? I pray Charlotte to be released of his clutches, and, if necessary, he come into me for the remainder of my days.'

'*Ohh!*' the multitude cried, surprising me. They were listening. I looked to Charlotte to see if she had heard them. She was still conversing with the women caring for her, oblivious to this heavy talk.

'Indeed,' continued Ainm. 'Such great love have we

not seen but rarely in the realm of mankind.' He bowed
to me, and it was then I noticed the wolves had lifted
their right paws in respect. 'Your prayer shall be
answered this night, save Gloom possessing you, which
we shall not allow. I regret to tell you, my lord, that you
must witness the death of your girl.'

Each of my arms were then grasped as if by iron
bands. 'No!' I screamed aloud, but Charlotte was already
in the midst of the wolves, and before my eyes she was
mercilessly torn apart by them until her body lay in
shreds.

'It is done,' stated Ceannaire, my Charlotte's blood
painting his cruel maw and dripping to the floor. I drew
my rapier and ran at the beast, blind with rage. I was
halted by a spike-haired warrior who looked kindly upon
me, yet stood resolute in his duty to halt me.

'Sir,' said Ainm to me aloud. 'Be patient. We have
set the girl free of the Devil, as your people sometimes
call him. *The Adversary. Satan. Azazel.* This be a day to
mark and celebrate. Be patient. She shall rise again to
life this very night.'

I stood swaying in delirium. 'The Devil? Satan?
No!— *no!* Azazel is bound in chains in Tartarus! It was
Gloom! She was merely possessed by the wayward spirit
calling himself Gloom, you outrageous fools! And, the
murdering Orange is yet inhabiting her— or was— *oh*

my dear God! What have you done? *Blue bottles on a stool!* What have you filthy sods done to my precious Charlotte!' I fell forward then and wept until I ached all over, and knew my heart would be torn asunder with the anguish I knew. No one came to comfort me. I would have accepted no soothing from this ignominious court anyway.

†

I awoke, bellowing, from a sleep filled with images of Charlotte being torn asunder by rabid wolves, by flatulent demons with green putrid hairless hides, by black-toothed ne'er-do-wells jumping from behind trees long dead, by my *own* fingers and incisors!

Breathing deeply in an attempt to awaken fully, I found that I was dressed in a white silken nightgown and lying on a bed made of down. The entire *décor* of the room was white like frost, and sunlight played into the chamber through a window covered in several layers of gauze curtains. Next to me was another bed. There lay Charlotte— whole again in limb and countenance, and sleeping soundly. On a wee table at the foot of her bed sat a wooden container like unto no handmade receptacle I had ever before seen, for its shape was pyramidal in design.

A maiden floated into our room then. I say she floated, for from where I lay I could plainly view the floor, and her legs did not at all move. She radiated an earthy scent both flowery and pungent. 'Wake up, wake up, wake up!' spoke she in a voice filled with playful delight, and then she vanished like mist.

Charlotte awoke, and lay astonished until she found me next to her. She began to weep. I went to her, and held her, and with great difficulty kept my own tears at bay.

'Where are we, Mister Coachman? Is this fairyland?'

'Indeed. I do believe this is fairyland. I am so happy you are alive.'

'Those wolves scared me, but their bites didn't hurt at all, and then— and then I fell asleep.'

With the memory of her vicious rending yet fresh in my memory, I could contain my tears no more as I pulled her to me. She wept the more then, and there we lay, arm in arm, weeping together, yet no longer captives.

'Azazel— *Satan*— is in this vessel,' a familiar voice informed. We looked. It was Ainm caressing the unique container on the table. 'Your horses are well rested, shoed anew, and fed. You may leave *this* way.' With a brush of his hand we were no longer in the sunny chamber, but standing, fully dressed in clean garments, upon the field where we were first encountered by the Cumhacht. We were alone. A table filled with hearty breakfast foods stood before us on the field. As our horses grazed, we ate to our hearts' content.

✝

'Take me home, Mister Coachman!'

A blade to my throat furthered the point.

'*Orange!*' I cried.

'It's *Pinprick*, you stupid sodder! Lift me up on my mount!'

I did as I was commanded, my mind grasping at new ideas, old ones, discarded ones— all carrying design of ridding us both of this inhuman possession. For, aye, indeed: I too had been possessed; and perhaps worse, was yet oppressed and hag-ridden by Lady Charlotte Proorice.

✝

We arrived to our cottage at twilight.

At dawn the smell of freshly spilt blood awakened me with a start.

In the main room I found horror anew, for there Charlotte knelt feasting on the uncooked flesh of a shepherd. 'I told you I need meat.' She did not look up from her lurid breakfast.

The lance I took from the mantle pierced only pierced her sleeve. Her dirk, however, lodged itself firmly in the muscle of my left shoulder. It was then that she returned to her hellish meal.

134

I found myself out of commission for a fortnight, during which time I spoke not a word to Charlotte. Soon my wound began to heal over, and inside two months time my arm, though a bit sore, had returned to regular use. In the mean time I was forced to endure two more human deaths (one shepherd, one roving fisherman) and the stealing of four sheep (of which I refused to partake). I found myself at wit's end. Was I deranged for not taking her life as she slept? I would deserve whatever punishment was given her should we be caught. Our one succor was the people's fear of *Gleann na Gruagh;* the fear of the fierce highwaymen abiding there.

The ghost was perhaps our only chance. The ghost of my voice. Orange, that foul presence, had to be driven out of her, for he was proving himself the equal of Captain Malvapor. There was no other way to save either of us. How would I proceed? I had to find Charlotte when Orange left her for a time. I had to watch her; watch her facial expressions and how she chose to relate to me. Orange never climbed into my lap. Orange never lay his head upon my shoulder. Orange never wrapped his arms about me. Orange never kissed me. Orange was not warm in the least. He was cold, calculating, and surely one of the Devil's right-hand men. *Ha*! The Devil! The Fallen Angel now trapped in a wooden pyramid by fairyfolk! Now I had seen everything.

I mused upon the Devil in his fairy-trap, and upon how it made no difference, apparently, that he had been taken from mankind, for I was sure that wars continued and strife did abound. What his influence, as 'Gloom,' had been against Ainm and his people must have been unspeakable for them to take such outlandish measures for his capture. Yet, though Charlotte and I had both suffered greatly for their hunt, I was glad for the fairyfolk— if that is what they were— and I sensed that Charlotte felt the same. I was, in the end, content that we had been able to assist them— assist us all, really, against the arch-enemy of all that is good and true in the world. Our own serenity, however, was again seeming out of reach.

†

'I can't reach you. Come get your food, wee squirrel! *Closer!*'

I looked round. I heard Charlotte, but where *was* she? 'Pinprick?'

She giggled. 'Up here, Mister Coachman! Up here in this ash tree! See me?'

Locating her, I smiled, and she blew a kiss toward me. Then she lost her footing, and fell backward and out of the tree, striking the back of her neck upon a gnarled root.

I ran to her, but her eyes were already closing.

'I love you, Mister Coachman. Please call me *Charlotte* one last time.'

'Oh, Charlotte! Don't leave me! Oh, my love, my Charlotte! *Oh, my dear God in Heaven—*'

'He hears you, Mister Coachman. He loves you, Mister Coachman. And— I love him— I love Jesus— Goodbye, Mister Coachman—'

'Goodbye, Charlotte— goodbye— oh, goodbye—'

And then in my arms she died.

8

Requiescat In Pace

I knew not what to feel or do when Charlotte left me. I sought to pen my thoughts, my feelings, down onto paper. The walls of our cottage are forever ink-stained with the result of that futile effort. Then, with paint and canvas procured from a robbery past I sought to illustrate my pain— to no avail worth speaking of. Then I sought to sing my feelings, my sorrow. No words would form, no melody could be produced from my wracked soul. So, I prayed. But the sky was brass. I sought the face of Jesus that much harder, and finally, after much travail, on my knees broken and in a flood of tears, he came to comfort me, and comforts me to this day.

The moment Charlotte's spirit passed from her body— remember that I was holding her when this occurred— I knew that my stint as a highwayman was done. What would I do? I gave that notion little thought. Life is not to be given to worry, but is for, as the Greeks say, *thinamis*. *Power*. Did Saint Paul warn that he would go back to the Corinthian church to argue theology with them? To try and coerce them with soft words? Or perhaps with dismissals of certain teachings which caused the most trouble among them? No! The Apostle

warned that should he need to travel back to them
because of their disobedience to the good news of eternal
life, he would go in power!

I had enough food and firewood cut to last me at
least half a year, but I would not remain hidden away in
the glen for a fraction of that time. On a day not long
after her death, a day when the birds and other forest
animals seemed to me to be particularly happy, I lay
Charlotte in an unmarked grave on the western slope of
the glen, covering her body with wood and stones
against wild animals before covering her with earth. I
believed then, as I do now, that I would see her again
one day.

Upon leaving the Glen of the Downs, I walked the
high road of the Wicklow Mountains as far as I could
toward Dublin, and then was careful to keep myself
incognito until I could get passage to London— which
was not at all difficult given the coinage I carried in my
purse. Ship captains vary from temperament to
temperament, but gold speaks louder than letters of
introduction, and certainly with more authority than
carefully crafted lies. My way having been attained with
little complexity, as part of my arrangement I served as a
swab so as not to arouse suspicions of the crew. The
captain was mercenary enough to keep our secret (upon
my promise of double my passage price into his private

coffer upon arrival in London), my low-estate ploy proved fruitful, I made a number of new friends aboardship on that brief journey from Dublin to Liverpool, and, as I pen this memoir a scant three months since the accident, I am situated— not also without the help of my wee golden friends— in a very good house in London, serving as head steward and tutor of children.

It is not my intent for anyone to read, and God forbid *publish*, these papers until after my death, whenever that may happen. I have always felt that I would live to be quite old. That may prove to be the case, and again, I may slip away in my sleep tonight. Every moment, I have come to understand— and certainly not without the unconscious help of Pinprick while she was yet living— is a gift to be used for the love of God, and for nothing else. I must pour myself out until there is nothing left of me to pour. He is my source of strength; he will renew me in his love, and rejoice over me with shouts of joy.

The remaining blood-money on my person I have given to the poor and needy under cover of night, whilst dressed to the hilt as a 'gentleman of the road' so as to discourage any comers who may carry devious intention. Sometimes our pasts come in rather handy.

Scáth Beorh, a former denizen of Ireland as well as other exhilarating parts of the world, has made the goal of his life to explore, to understand the fallen human condition. Some artists work in paints, others in wood or stone, leather or iron. Beorh works in words. More can be found about this writer at **twelvehousebooks.wordpress.com** or he may be written to personally via **beorh.house@gmail.com**